SACRIFICE

I0618201

LOLA
TAYLOR

Though several weeks have passed since her family's murder, werewolf queen Alara Crescent can't seem to let go of the pain. It's festered inside of her like a disease, twisting her thoughts until the only thing she can seem to think about is revenge. It doesn't help that her dead sister keeps visiting her in her dreams, warning her of an approaching threat that could tear her new pack apart…

Nik knows his mate has changed. Gone is the unsure-of-herself princess, replaced by a werewolf queen with an appetite for blood. Not that he, of all people, can't appreciate that, but he wants his mate back.

When a doppelgänger stumbles into a pack celebration, Nik and Alara know it's more than a coincidence. Doppelgängers are bad luck, rumored to make people insane with rage and bloodthirst, on top of being creepy as hell. But no sweat for Nik and Alara. They think they have the problem—aka, "one unwelcome body snatcher"—taken care of when they send the doppelgänger away with the DPI, but their problems are only just beginning. One by one, their pack members fall prey to something sinister, and Alara's own demons become restless, turning her into a deadly vixen that could rival the vilest and most dangerous denizens of the Underworld. She wants answers to her family's senseless murders—now.

And she'll do anything to get them.

Will Nik be able to break the curse of the doppelgänger in time to save his mate before her soul is lost to the darkness forever?

Cover designed by Kitten of Deranged Doctor Design
Interior design and formatting by
Copy Edited by Susie of Red Adept Editing
Proofread by Kim of Red Adept Editing
Indigo Dreamer Press logo designed by Indi99o of 99designs
Author photograph by Sara Rogers Photography

www.lolataylorbooks.com
www.indigodreamerpress.com

INDIGO
DREAMER PRESS

ISBN-10: 0-9835131-9-8
ISBN-13: 978-0-9835131-9-3

For more information, please visit
www.lolataylorbooks.com

CHAPTER ONE

Alara arched her back and moaned as Nik's tongue raked over her sex.

He squeezed her plush hips, making her open her legs wider as he went deeper. She whimpered, her nails digging into the fur rug that lay sprawled before the massive fireplace in their bedroom.

No one would dare disturb them, so she relished the moment. Every second, every breath, every heartbeat. Modesty be damned, especially when he was doing *this* with his mouth.

Her whole body came alive as Nik kissed her most sensitive spot then licked her body from her navel to the dip in her throat. "You are so beautiful," he said as he kissed her neck, his voice husky with want.

He slowly rocked into her as he said it, pushing inside just enough to make her gasp—then growl as he slid back out. "Tease," she said, nipping at his lower lip as she hid a

1

smile.

He raised a brow, a mischievous sparkle to his eyes. "Never. I'm just enjoying myself. Shouldn't a wolf want to enjoy his mate?"

"You've been enjoying me for the past twenty minutes," she said with a wicked grin of her own.

He paused, still grinning as if he could read her mind. "You're saying you didn't enjoy it?"

"I'm saying," she purred, grabbing hold of his cock and positioning it against her sex, "that I'm growing restless." She grabbed hold of his tight ass and pressed downward.

He might be her Alpha, but in the bedroom she was the master. And judging by how hard he was, he was just as eager for her.

He plunged into her. A contented sigh escaped her as exquisite fire bloomed deep below her navel. She brought her hips up to meet his as he began picking up a familiar rhythm. Their bodies rocked together as they made love, their hips rising and falling as the flames within her grew.

She closed her eyes. Ah, there it was—emotion. She hadn't tasted it in so long, she'd almost forgotten what it felt like to *feel*. It was intoxicating, her senses coming alive with her soul's thirst to be whole, to feel normal, again. "Faster," she breathed, digging her nails into his back.

He obeyed, but she could tell he was still holding back.

Something about that set her teeth to grinding. She growled low in her throat. "Harder," she clipped, her breathlessness making the command harsher than she intended.

His rhythm stumbled before he at last stopped. He lay

on top of her, panting hard. Sweat was starting to bead on his skin, making the valley of hard muscles on his body shine in the orange firelight that bathed their room. The indigo ink of their mate-bond tattoos shimmered, a thousand tiny blue crystals twinkling with the reflection of orange flame.

Her brows furrowed as she studied his face. She swallowed her frustration. "What's wrong?" she asked, brushing the wisps of hair out of his face. He'd started to grow it out since they'd gotten back to Crescent Manor a few weeks ago. She had to admit, it made him look boyishly cute, though it had taken some getting used to.

Nik sighed and sat up on his elbows, so he straddled either side of her head. "Nothing's wrong, love."

She blinked, idly playing with damp pieces of his bangs. He was hiding something. It was in the way he ducked his head, not quite looking at her when he spoke. She'd have to be gentle so as to coax it out of him. "Then why did you stop?"

He caught her hand and gently kissed her knuckles. She tried to catch her wince but wasn't fast enough.

"Exactly because of that," he said quietly, examining the backs of her hands. They looked a hell of a lot different than when she was a princess. Thanks to the angry red scabs and bruises, she looked as if she punched concrete on a daily basis. It about felt like that now, but she was starting to form calluses. Once she would have balked at the idea of having "man's hands," but now she was rather proud of them. They made her feel strong, more in control. Beating the shit out of a punching bag was about the only time she felt any semblance of control.

More scars to match the rest.

Her mate studied her, gently playing with her hair. He liked to do that. While they spoke, tangled in each other's arms in bed, he'd often run his fingers through her hair. She couldn't say she objected.

Nik watched her warily, trying to be so careful. Which, in itself, was damn impressive, considering he usually spewed whatever thought came to mind without any filter. "I hear you slipping out of bed every morning before dawn," he said quietly, "and your scent is all over the training room. You haven't given yourself one break since we've been back." Pause—cue a deep breath. "I wish you wouldn't be so hard on yourself," he added, more softly and with a hint of sadness.

Her heart wrenched with an unfamiliar twist of regret.

And rage. That emotion, that simmering, restless anger, had been her one constant. She was mad as hell, a ticking time bomb. She had been ever since her family's deaths. Training and trying to relieve the anger with physical exertion was the only way she knew how to exorcise the pain.

She opened her mouth to tell Nik just that and then choked. God, why did she always choke? Why was it so hard to talk about this?

Feeling as if her throat were closing up, she blinked and looked away. *Coward.* "Who says I'm being hard on myself? Werewolf packs need strong queens. Everyone here is a way better warrior than I am. I want to get better. I want to get stronger."

He grinned. "Way better, huh? Humph. That's the first time I've heard you not speak in perfectly polite sentences." He poked her on the tip of her nose. "Your 'poshness' is wearing off, Your Highness."

"Well, look at the company I keep."

He snorted and pulled her closer. "I'm ruining you."

"It was bound to happen."

She smiled. The motion still felt stiff. Fake. It was also usually accompanied by a wave of guilt and a little annoying voice that preached how she shouldn't be happy. That she didn't have the right to be happy when her family was dead.

When her little sister, so innocent and kind and everything she wasn't, was now cold in her grave.

She shivered as her blood turned to ice.

Nik rubbed her arms as goose bumps broke out over her skin. Mmmmmm, he was so warm. Though her temperature ran naturally hot too, she still loved snuggling next to her mate's gorgeous bared body.

Nik rested his head on hers. For a pensive moment, the only sounds in the room were their beating hearts and the gentle swish of their breathing. "Beating the pain out of yourself isn't going to make it go away," he said, his breath ruffling her hair. "It'll only remind you of why you're there and make you angrier."

Her fists tightened. *I couldn't possibly be any angrier.* She couldn't say it out loud, couldn't ever acknowledge that sleeping beast. For if she did, she didn't know if she'd be able to control it.

"I should know," he went on thoughtfully. "I got in a

lot of fights growing up."

"But you didn't have a choice." She didn't need to look at the network of scars along his body to make her point; they spoke for themselves. "You said you had to protect your little brother. And your father," she added bitterly. It was a good thing he was already dead—otherwise, she might have to assassinate the son of a bitch. Anyone who hurt her Nik, father-in-law or not, automatically went onto her shit list.

"Yeah, but I still felt pissed off all the time because of the pain inside." He smiled sadly at her. "Sometimes you don't realize how much you care about people until they're gone."

The tension and ice that had been draining out of her returned. She could feel her shoulders knotting up.

God, what did she think about losing her family? Hell if she knew. Even after weeks of diary therapy and "therapist" therapy, she was still no closer to figuring out the tangle of emotions inside of her. All she knew was she was sick of feeling hurt. And numb. Or crazy pissed off. It was always one of the three. Either she hurt like hell, or she didn't hurt at all.

Except when she had sex with Nik. It felt *so damn good* to be with him, to give herself over to her more carnal nature.

Unfortunately, Nik had started catching on. He hadn't said anything about it yet, but he'd started cutting their sexcapades short.

He rolled over onto his back and patted his chest. She curled up next to him, laying her head against his beating heart. "I'm sorry," she said softly, staring at the crackling flames.

"Don't be," he said, kissing her forehead. "I know."

She smiled her broken smile. Hey, it might have been broken, but at least it still worked. That had to mean something. Maybe she wasn't completely unfixable.

Or she was a damn optimistic idiot.

She heaved a shaky sigh as the fear that she'd never feel like herself again returned. A moment later, as if out of some natural instinct of self-preservation, the numbness started to take over. Call her a coward, but she let it. Every. Single. Time. Because feeling nothing was easier than trying to face the real problem—why she gave a damn her father and mother were gone in the first place.

She cleared her throat, mostly so she could swallow again. Her throat had gotten so tight, it was even getting difficult to breathe. "What time are Gage and Danica coming over?" she asked, ready to change the subject.

Distractions were her other means of coping, whether it be in the form of a book, exploring the manor, or whatever else she could come up with. Long, empty periods of time to just think, think, think and worry, worry, worry were her enemies. "Just stay busy," her therapist had said. "It'll help with the depression." Alara didn't think she could get any more depressed than she already was, but hey, she wasn't the licensed shrink.

"Noon," Nik said, glancing at the clock over the mantel. "And I have some new real estate contracts to look over, as well as some bills to discuss with our treasurer before then."

The Moonstruck Pack was run much like any other organization. Some pack masters made their mates their Betas, but not Nik. He'd surprised everyone by claiming dual leadership, making her his equal in every way. Dual Alphas were nearly unheard of in the Underworld. She was always included at every meeting, her opinion weighed in on every decision. It meant so much to her that Nik would stop at nothing to include her in his life, to make this pack mean more to her than she'd meant to her last one.

Which was nothing other than a pawn.

Being crown princess had felt a lot like wearing shackles, but not here. Here, she was a queen in her own right, and the pack treated her as such.

So why couldn't she just be happy?

Alara sighed. "Do we have to get up?"

"Afraid so, love." He kissed her head again, and together they rose. They went over pack business as they showered and got dressed for the day. It was a familiar routine, and familiar was comforting. She started to relax and not feel quite so on edge and lost. Nik seemed to sense her need for distraction, and she appreciated it.

He kissed her at the door. "Leave some of those punching bags for me later, killer."

"I wouldn't be much of a killer if I did," she said coyly over her shoulder.

He laughed. "That's my girl."

She smiled at him as he went one way and she another, decked out in her favorite sweats, sneakers, and tank top. Such tight-fitting clothes would have made her uncomfortable before, considering her curves. Nik was slowly starting to help her overcome that. He worshiped her body, saying he preferred her soft curves to cutting himself on the skin-and-bone she-wolves he'd dated. And besides, considering everything that had happened, worrying about her appearance seemed... silly. Trivial, even. There were so many larger things at play here, things that demanded her attention.

Like kicking the shit out of a punching bag before she turned into a green rage monster.

Before she reached the stairs, a catcall sounded from across the hall.

She made a little show of shaking her hips for her mate and grinned when he chuckled a moment later.

God, she loved that man. Maybe a little too much.

He could be taken from you just as easily.

No. No, that was the one thought she could never, ever think. It was bad luck. Had to be, as if even thinking it would make it come true.

Curses be damned. This girl was getting her shit together.

She marveled at how much she had changed on her way to the gym. Gone was the perfect little princess. In her body was a proud, sassy woman ready to take charge of her life.

She just had some anger issues to sort out first. Okay, so maybe a lot of anger issues, but that was what the punching bags were for.

There was just enough time for a brief thirty-minute workout before she had to get ready for her morning meetings. There was a lot to do before the High King and Queen of Werewolves made a visit to them, most of which she was in charge of. It made her feel proud to be trusted with all these responsibilities, and she took her job seriously. She was determined to do her best. No one in the pack would respect her if she behaved like a spoiled lapdog. The days of being "seen not heard" were over. Now, she proudly earned her keep. It was so nice to be thought of as more than a puppet.

She arrived at the massive gymnasium and turned on the lights. It was underground, so it stayed nice and cool. Mirrors lined every wall, and large TVs and expensive stereo systems dotted the corners. Most of the time she didn't even turn the TV or stereo on, but today she needed more distraction.

Nik scraping the topic that was the real source of her problems had set her on edge more than she cared to admit. Not to mention that remembering who was visiting them today reminded her of the titles her deceased family had previously held. She knew she'd go mad if she were forced to think of them for long.

Don't be a time bomb. Work it out.

Settling in to her routine, she wrapped up the sensitive, broken skin along her knuckles and took up a defensive stance in front of her favorite punching bag. She pictured the face of Gerard, of all the snotty-nosed brats at the palace, and everyone else who'd ever shunned her or let her down. She hit as hard as she could, pouring all her negative energy into the bag as her therapist had instructed.

All of her anger came to a boil, rising up from the dungeon she kept it chained in and making her skin burn. She bared her teeth, and she snarled at the bag as her frustration built.

Damn you, Gerard.

Damn you, Mistress Black.

Damn you, Order.

Damn, damn, damn.

It started out as the prickling of hairs along her arms and neck and then turned into the heightened sense of being watched. A shadow swept past the door. She'd been so caught up in her anger that she'd almost missed it. Catching the movement in the mirror, she whirled, eyes searching the dark hallway.

She waited, wolf ears pricked and listening for footsteps over the chatter of the TV.

There. Someone was walking away.

As quietly as she could, she approached the door. Grabbing one of the knives she still had yet to learn to use properly from the weapons rack, she braced herself and stepped into the hall. She glanced first to the left, then to the right, then back again.

It was empty.

And yet the signature of something she'd never felt before lingered in the hall.

Her heart was beating faster when she went back inside the gym. It was keycard-entry only, with solid steel doors reinforced by spells and wards, so it wasn't as though just anyone could bust in.

Yet she found she couldn't shake her discomfort as

she resumed her position at her bag. Cursing herself for being such a coward, she went to the opposite side of the bag, putting the door right in her line of vision.

As well as anyone who might be watching her.

CHAPTER TWO

Nik Johnson fucking hated meetings. Since he was a pack master, however, they were a necessary evil.

When he thought his head couldn't possibly be crammed full of any more nonsense about real estate, a welcome knock came at the door to the meeting hall. He glanced at his watch. It was scuffed as hell, but that was what he loved about it. They'd been through shit together. He'd never been the type to splurge on pricey shit just for the hell of it. "Pricey" often meant "status symbol" to him, and he fucking hated that shit. Living in a manor had always set him ill at ease too, but at least he had a roof over his head.

Nik wrapped up the meeting and adjourned the three men before him. Sometimes running the pack felt more like being the president of a very rowdy private club. They had a president (him), VP (his Beta), a treasurer, a scribe, and so on. They met once a week to discuss pack business and get their affairs in order.

Definitely not the rock-star life he'd imagined as a kid.

After everyone had cleared out, a throat cleared, and Nik looked up to see who had rapped at the door.

The werewolf stopped before him and bowed his head. He wore jeans and a T-shirt, the unofficial uniform of the Moonstruck Pack. Nik really should make them clean up and look like respectable werewolves, but he couldn't bring himself to give a damn. It was the least of his mounting concerns.

The werewolf smacked his fist over his heart, the token sign of respect and loyalty among the pack. "Sire, the High King is here."

Nik had to resist the urge to growl. Now he knew exactly how irritated his brother had felt when called "Your Highness," "Sire," "Exalted One," and whatever title Nik could come up with just to needle Gage. "Thank you," he said, forcing his lips to stretch in a tight smile. "I will meet with him in the drawing room."

The drawing room was just a fancy phrase for Nik's office, but it was still fun to say it. He smiled inside. Maybe some of Alara had rubbed off on him after all.

His office had made quite the change since Malachite's reign. For one, there were no longer skulls and stuffed wolf heads in there. The whole thing had been fucking morbid, and he'd torn it all down and completely remodeled it first thing. Well, actually, Gage had done that. He couldn't stand it either.

While Gage's tastes were more muted than Nik's, the office was functional. No bells, no whistles, no fancy pencil sharpener, because let's admit it, who the hell still used pencil sharpeners? Nope, just plain and simple. Nik had, however, indulged himself in adding pictures of motorcycles everywhere, along with some motorcycle knick-knacks just for the hell of it. He had to make the office his somehow. Telling himself it was because he was a werewolf and they marked their territory was how he'd justified buying all that shit.

He followed Bracken, an older werewolf who looked as if he'd been a stoner in the seventies, into the office. The manor was crawling with more watchful werewolf eyes; Gage's royal guards had apparently had no problem dispersing themselves in strategic positions. Everyone seemed wary but civil, at least. It was the best he could hope for in any event combining werewolves from two different packs.

A pair of guards—his, judging from the holey, torn jeans and all-around "thug" look—opened his office doors. He strolled in, the office stretching before him. It was long and big, no pun intended, at least twenty by thirty feet. He had a sitting area with some comfortable leather furniture, since no man cave was complete without it. Considering he practically lived here, or in the bedroom with his mate, this was as close to a man cave as he was going to get.

The other half of the office housed his massive oak desk and row upon row of shelves filled with books, files, and other important documents.

A tall man stood to greet him.

A smile immediately spread across Nik's face. "How's the first month in office treating you, Your Highness?"

"You're never going to stop calling me that, are you?" Gage said, smiling widely as the two brothers embraced.

One of the royal guards still lingered nearby and cleared his throat.

Gage held up a hand. "It's all right. He doesn't have to bow and all that."

Nik grinned. Gage was already turning out to be a fine king. He leaned in, keeping his voice low. "About damn time we put someone on the throne with an even head on his shoulders."

Gage's eyes shone with pride. His eyes cut to his guard, who looked ready to draw his gun on Nik. "It's fine. Tell the others to see that my queen is okay. You are dismissed."

The guard looked uncomfortable at leaving but obeyed. Once the doors were shut and they were alone, they relaxed their shoulders. Gage closed his eyes and sighed. No one would guess by looking at his button-up plaid shirt, jeans, and boots that he was a king.

"It's so good to be back," he said, glancing around. "I see you've redecorated. Have you taken Alara out for any bike rides yet?"

"A few," Nik said. "She still wants to hold on too tight around curves."

"And that's a problem?" Gage asked with a suggestive smile.

Nik snorted. "Nah. You know how I am." Which was perpetually horny. He definitely wasn't complaining about feeling Alara's generous breasts bunched up against his back whenever they went for bike rides. It took everything in him not to pull over and tug her into the woods on some of their longer rides.

Gage's eyes lingered about the room, and his smile slanted sadly.

Nik didn't need him to explain. He walked up to his brother and grasped his arms, squeezing. "This is still your home too. Anytime you need to get away."

Gage's smile broadened. "Thank you, brother."

Nik gave him a gruff nod. It felt a little weird not seeing his brother in a month. He'd always been looking out for him, always protected him, but now he had an army to do that. The sting of being unwanted was tough at first—until Nik realized how fucking stupid that was. It wasn't as if Gage were a toy that only Nik could play with. He was a High King now, with responsibilities. Both were now kings in their own rights.

Though Nik loathed the political bullshit that went along with the title, he vowed to be the best damn king he could. His brother had entrusted him with this gig, and no way in hell could he let Gage down and make him look bad.

Gage seemed just as uncomfortable in the awkward silence as Nik. He shifted his weight around and smiled.

Time to break the ice.

"Want a drink?" Nik asked, heading to the beverage counter.

"Would I ever," Gage said, following behind.

Nik poured the two wolves four fingers of whiskey, and they sat down together on the leather furniture.

The two brothers sat in silence for a moment before Nik cleared his throat. "Well, since you know I'm not one to beat around the bush, I'm guessing you didn't drop out of paradise just to say hello."

Gage smiled. There was a tightness to it that set Nik's wolf senses on edge.

Gage stared into his drink, swirling the glass's contents. "I talked to Verika."

Well, that wasn't anything unusual. "And?"

When Gage didn't look at him, Nik sat up. "Spit it out, bro. What's eating you?"

Gage went still. When he lifted his gaze, it was as hard as stone. "Elijah is still alive."

Nik thought he couldn't possibly have heard him correctly. He snorted and blinked, settling back on the cushions as he took a long swig of his whiskey. "Yeah, right. That son of a bitch ended up in a ditch a long time ago. Had to have, with the type of company he liked to keep."

No, that last part didn't sound bitter at all, his inner prick drawled.

"It's the truth."

When Gage didn't once crack a smile, the giggles drained right out of Nik. A chill went through him. "You shitting me?"

"No," Gage said roughly, downing the rest of his alcohol. "Never about this."

Holy fucking shit. Elijah—Eli—was alive.

Nik had no idea how to begin to process how he felt about that. Relieved? Pissed off? Angry? It wasn't anger at Elijah being alive, per se, as much as anger that the asshole was alive and hadn't bothered saying anything to them about it.

How long had it been since they'd spoken? Years? Their childhood felt like a lifetime ago. Hell, it was a whole other life ago. They'd been completely different boys then.

Now, they were men with baggage.

Fuck.

Every curse word Nik knew spewed out of his mouth. He stood, pacing and still swearing.

Gage stood with him. "Verika called when Danica and I were in Colorado," he started. "I would have called to tell you, but it didn't seem like the type of thing you casually spoke of on the phone. I needed to tell you in person."

No shit. He might have been tempted to blow it off as a lie or an ill-suited joke had Gage spouted this off on the phone.

Gage launched into the conversation he and Verika had had, how he'd picked apart everything she'd said. Nik knew Verika well enough to know she'd never joke around about something like this.

He felt as if someone had punched him in the gut and knocked the wind out of him. The itch to drink burned his throat more than the whiskey did as he gulped it down like water. Before he could squeeze it any tighter and break it, he set his empty glass down and gripped the back of the couch. "Fuuuuuuuuuuccccccckkkkk." He heard the tear of leather. His nails had sharpened into claws as his inner wolf momentarily took over.

Calming himself, he released the couch and ran his hands through his hair. It still felt weird actually having hair to get in his eyes, but Alara seemed to like it. "Fuck."

"You've said that already," Gage teased lightly.

"I don't know what else to say." Nik let his arms flop back to his sides before he fell back on the couch like a rock. He stared into empty space. Oh yeah. The realization that Elijah was alive had fried his brain, all right.

Gage slowly sat, eyeing Nik warily.

Shit. "What now?" Nik asked, noting the edge in his voice.

"There's more, about the pack," Gage said carefully, leaning forward. "Brace yourself."

Two words Nik never liked to hear. "What is it?"

Two minutes later, he was taking the whiskey straight from the bottle.

CHAPTER THREE

FRIENDS WERE WEIRD.

Well, not that *her* friends were weird, but rather, the fact that she had any at all floored Alara.

She listened with rapt interest as Danica chattered (read: "bitched") about all the snobs at the castle. Alara laughed, feeling genuinely relaxed around Danica as the two women walked toward the open field behind the manor, where a banquet was to be held in the High King and Queen's honor.

"I'm glad to see some things never change," Alara said wryly.

"Ugh. Oh my gosh." Danica rolled her eyes, and Alara bit back a smile. It was such an un-Queen-like thing to do. "They're just jerks, you know? I just want to say, 'Okay, I know I'm not born and bred were royalty, and you think you're better than me, but really you're not, because I can totally have you beheaded… or something.'"

Alara laughed. "I'm sure you'll strike terror into the hearts of all your enemies, Your Highness."

"Stop calling me that." Danica swatted Alara's arm. "It's weird enough hearing it around the castle all day. It's totally unacceptable coming from you, Miss Perfect."

Alara raised a brow. "I'm perfect?"

"Uh-huh." Danica nodded. "Totally, irritatingly perfect. We need to work on your slovenliness so I don't feel like such a disaster waiting to happen."

Alara thought of all the blood she wished to spill in her family's name, of the darkness stirring inside of her like a caged beast. A knot formed in her chest, and she ducked her head. "I'm not a saint. Believe me."

Danica snorted. "Yeah, right. If you're not a saint, then what the hell does that make me?"

On their way to the door, they passed by the long, weapon-adorned wall that lay parallel to one of the meeting rooms.

Alara stared at it often. She couldn't help it; something about the hint of violence stole her attention, especially since she'd been training. She never used to pay weapons any mind, maybe even feared them, but now she was enraptured.

A machete caught her eye. Alara stared at the blade hanging on the wall. It was one of many used to decorate Crescent Manor, and she didn't know exactly why this one had drawn her gaze. Perhaps it was the wicked curve of the blade or the row of sharp teeth waiting to slice through warm flesh.

Oh, what she'd give to watch it saw through Gerard's

neck…

"Alara?"

She blinked.

Danica looked at her expectantly, waiting a few steps ahead. "Something wrong?"

Alara shook her head and pasted on a smile. "No, I'm fine. Thanks." She started walking again, picking up the easy conversation where they'd left off, though Danica still cast her an odd, curious look every now and then.

The moon was out tonight. The nearly full, brilliant-white orb shone bright against a backdrop of stars. Their breaths puffed in the air as Danica and Alara walked over toward the large campfire that had been set ablaze about fifty feet from the house.

A circular stone courtyard surrounded the fire pit. People milled about, laughing, talking, and drinking. A huge buffet had been set up on a long table off to the side, right next to a mountain of kegs. Werewolves loved the shit out of some beer. The Moonstruck Pack had spared no expense in making the High Royalty feel welcome.

Despite the laughter, Alara felt a thread of tension riding the air.

Not all the wolves had forgiven Gage for what had happened at the cabin in the woods. Many of those who'd been slain by the wraiths were longtime friends. That kind of grief took a long time to go away, if ever. The resentment and bitterness it brought on would take even longer to fade. The thirst for revenge, the itch to make someone pay, was like a stain that wouldn't fade.

Alara should know. Her entire soul was bathed in her

desire for revenge.

Shoving her anger and pain inside, she took her place beside her mate and forced a smile as formalities were quickly dispensed with.

Yeah, the applause as the High King and Queen were officially announced was definitely lackluster.

The discontentment in the pack was a growing problem that had been on their radar right from the start. If it was left unchecked, they may very well have a mutiny on their hands. The murderous gleam she caught in the pack's eyes as they watched Gage, and sometimes Nik, definitely made her uneasy. She wondered how many stares she'd received.

If only she had eyes in the back of her head.

Her mind wandered to Nik, as it often did when she was seeking reassurance, whether subconsciously or otherwise. Their mate-bond felt strained. One look at him, and she knew why. Her mate seemed… tense. She watched his gait, studied the tilt of his shoulders for a few seconds. Yeah, something was definitely wrong. She wondered how the meeting with Gage had gone and if that was the source of the tension.

She was going to ask him about it when he turned to her. The instant his eyes laid on her, the tension in their bond, and in his posture, eased. Gage swept Danica away to greet the pack members they'd left behind, allowing Nik to give her his full attention now that the festivities were officially underway.

Nik came up behind her and wrapped his arms around her waist, kissing her cheek. "How's my favorite mate doing this evening?"

Alara raised a brow and smiled. "I'd better be your only mate."

Nik grabbed her chin, and she craned her neck to face him. "You know you're the only woman for me," he said, kissing her.

His tongue darted into her mouth, and she eagerly met it with a moan. The heat that had remained pooled between her legs from their last intimate moment surged upward. Discreetly, beneath the folds of her jacket, she palmed his growing erection.

He growled low in his throat. "Careful, love," he murmured in her ear. "You're tempting me to strip you down and take you right here."

"We could always slip away for a bit?" she whispered back. Her voice lifted upward on the end in a conspiratorial question.

Nik stared at her with pure hunger in his eyes. For any wolf, mated or not, a full moon promised that your sex drive would be insatiable.

Without another word, he silently took her hand and led her away from the crowd and into the woods.

Her heart raced faster, and her desire coated her sex as they walked. She couldn't wait to feel him inside of her. Pumping, driving himself to the brink of exhaustion...

The fire was still visible between the veil of trees. If anything happened, they could respond quickly. Sure, they were hosting, and it was probably rude to step out, but hell if she could wait a second longer to be with her mate. Besides, she had a feeling that as worked up as they both were, this wouldn't take long.

Regrettably.

Nik came to an abrupt halt. Alara barely had time to register what was happening as he caught her before she could slam into him. Like a professional dancer, he spun her around and gently laid her back against a tree as his mouth came down hard over hers.

Her brain switched off as carnal need took over. Answering his tongue with a fiery kiss of her own, she eagerly began undoing his pants. His hand slid up to cup her breast through the soft material of the shift dress. Despite the padding of her bra, he easily found her pert nipple, teasing it with the tips of his fingers.

She pressed her throbbing breasts against him. The feel of the bark scraping against the fabric of her dress only excited her more. He grabbed her ass, and she hoisted herself up, wrapping her legs around his waist.

He hiked up her dress, exposing her bare sex. His deep chuckle rolled through her as he stroked her bare skin. "No panties?" he murmured, kissing her neck and then punctuating the gesture with a light nip. "I am rubbing off on you."

"Not yet, but I'm hoping to change that in a moment." She grabbed his full erection and aimed the tip upward.

He bucked, driving himself into her. She threw back her head with a gasp as he filled her up and began pumping with urgency. The pleasure was exquisite.

He sucked on a nipple; he'd pried her dress, and her now slightly torn bra, halfway up her body until it had nearly come off.

"Yes," she breathed as her orgasm bubbled upward. "Yes, yes…"

She came with a barely muffled scream, having had enough mind to clamp her mouth shut and swallow the joy of coming undone. Every tendon tingled, every muscle went gooey at the intensity of the sensations rolling through her right now. The pleasure was made even more intense because it briefly shattered all the pain she'd been feeling, driving away the darkness and filling it with Nik's physical manifestation of love.

Nik growled deep in his throat, clinging to her and bucking hard. His hot seed poured into her, and she relished the feeling of being one with him.

Her mate. Her beautiful, sexy, perfect mate.

How did she get so lucky?

Both breathing hard, they rested their foreheads against one another's. "How do you feel?" he murmured.

"Content," she said breathlessly. She leaned forward and kissed him gently on the lips. Their skin was covered in a light sheen of sweat. A lump formed in her throat. "I'm sorry," she whispered.

Nik frowned. "For what?"

"For not appreciating what's right in front of me," she said carefully. "For living in the past."

"Sweetheart," he said, hugging her close. "I've lived in the past most of my life. It's all right. I know what it's like to be eaten alive by that kind of grief and bitterness. It will pass. I promise you, I'll help you through it every step of the way." He smiled as he cupped her face in his hands. "Don't ever apologize to me for feeling. You might be a wolf, but you're still human."

Tears pricked her eyes, and she smiled. "Nik—"

Both their heads snapped around as something crashed through the woods toward them. It didn't sound heavy enough to be an animal, but it also didn't give off a human or supernatural signature.

Nik instantly set her down and shielded her. He growled, his eyes glowing gold as she scrambled to get dressed.

The sounds were growing closer, and she peered around his shoulder. Neither of them spoke. Alara knew he was listening with as much intent with his wolf hearing as she.

The people at the party must have heard the intruder too, because several footsteps were thundering toward them.

A moment later, a silhouette appeared between a pair of trees. It was human, at least, or humanoid, but that could mean a lot of things in their world. A lot of creatures held human shapes, but that made them no less dangerous.

"Stop right there!" Nik demanded with a snarl. His eyes blazed gold, and his teeth were sharpened to fangs. He looked terrifying.

The creature gasped and stopped, holding up two arms. Flashlight beams shone through the darkness as the rest of their party crashed through the trees to join them.

"What happened?" asked Gage, surrounded by his guards.

Alara blushed. "Um—"

"We went off to find some privacy, and someone came

charging toward us," Nik said, having no qualms about telling his brother exactly what they had been doing. Alara, by far, had to be the most modest werewolf in existence.

Gage's stern face was all business. He nodded to his men, and the flashlight beams shone upward.

They landed on the face of a young woman, her hair coated in mud and twigs. She was covered in nothing more than a shabby blanket, her skin clinging so closely to her pronounced bones that it very well could have been painted on.

"Help me," she croaked, trembling. Tears ran down her face. The only way Alara could tell she had been crying was from the clean lines running down her cheeks, which otherwise were coated in mud.

Alara studied her for a few seconds as she reached out with her supernatural senses, all while a nagging voice in the back of her head screeched that something wasn't right. It took her a moment to put her paw on it. When she did, she barely contained her gasp.

The girl's signature… it was just like the one she'd sensed outside the gym earlier, when she thought someone had been watching her.

CHAPTER FOUR

WHAT. THE. FUCK?

Nik stared at the girl. She was pretty—and filthy as hell. She looked as if she'd been living in the forest for a while. Her odor definitely suggested "wild child."

She trembled once more as fresh tears ran rivers through the grime caked on her face. "Please, help me," she whispered again in broken syllables. Her voice was scratchy, as though she hadn't had water in days.

Or maybe from screaming.

And if she'd been screaming, why? Had someone done something to her? Was someone after her? If they were after her, then he needed to know why before he put his pack at risk. But he also couldn't just leave her here to fend for herself, not when she was clearly weakened.

Being a pack master seriously sucked sometimes.

Thanks, Gage.

Nik's jaw was set in a stern line as he tried to figure out

what the hell to do.

She looked innocent enough, but so did a lot of other shit that could rip your throat out and not bat a lash.

He lifted his chin and sniffed. For a split second, he thought his mind was playing tricks on him. Her paranormal signature danced and shifted, as if it couldn't quite decide what it was, before firmly snapping into that of a werewolf.

He put all his focus into studying her signature again. Yeah, she was definitely a werewolf.

Weird. Must be my imagination. That was, until his mate got inside his head, literally.

Did you feel her signature? Alara asked through their telepathic mate-bond.

Yeah, he said gravely, not looking at her. Natural "human" instinct was to look at the person you were talking to, but in certain situations it was best not to give away the fact that you were having a telepathic chat. *Ever felt anything like that before?*

No, she said, starting to shake her head but stopping herself. She shifted her weight, and Nik could tell she was hiding something. He did look at her then and narrowed his eyes.

What? he asked gently.

She bit her lip. *This morning, at the gym, I felt a presence like hers. It was odd, like it was every paranormal creature and nothing at all at the same time.*

Fuck.

There were a few dozen creatures that could cause that phenomenon, all of them bad news. He'd worry about figuring out what the hell the girl really was later. Right now, he was more interested in why the fuck she'd been snooping around his manor and, more specifically, his mate.

He made up his mind right then. "Take her prisoner," he said in a deep voice booming with authority.

The girl's eyes widened as two members of his pack stepped forward to seize her. "But I haven't done anything wrong!" she cried, her feeble voice cracking on the last word.

Nik paid the girl no sympathy as he stared back at her with an iron will in his eyes. "We shall see." He nodded his head, and his men gently led her from the forest and back into the manor. Gage and Danica were right there with them as they hauled the girl into the sparsely used holding cells below the ground level.

The dungeons had been very popular during Malachite's reign. Nik had spent time in them himself, bleeding from multiple wounds inflicted by Malachite as punishment for his insubordination.

Rest in peace, you son of a bitch... or not. Burn in hell was probably more appropriate.

The dull pang of guilt made that vicious thought pause.

When Gage told him about what the Moonstruck Pack had done to Malachite's family, Nik hadn't believed a word of it. Mostly, he knew, it was because he hadn't wanted to. Ignorance really was bliss.

As it was, the pack was ready to rip him and his brother a new one thanks to the wraith debacle. Tracking down the perpetrators of the murder of Malachite's family would take time and resources. The resources part they were fine on. If anything, the Moonstruck Pack had always handled their finances well, even in Malachite's days. He'd been more keen on bloodshed and gore than depleting the pack's money reserves. Plus, Gage was High King, which kind of made him one of the richest paranormals in the Underworld.

So, yeah, resources—check.

But the time-suck part of conducting an investigation was a problem. Even if he outsourced it, Nik knew he would want to follow up on every lead himself. Despite his irritation with all the stress that came with the title of Alpha, he would die before he let anything hurt his wolves. Slaughtering humans was a grave offense, usually taken up by the state, and possibly national, paranormal justice courts. The pack's views of him were lukewarm, at best, as it was. If he tried punishing them or even hinted at retribution for what they'd done, then life as he knew it might literally plunge straight into hell. But at the same time, he couldn't in good conscience let such a crime go unpunished, *if* some of the original murderers still lurked in his pack. Besides, in addition to letting that kind of filth stay in his pack, how long would it be before they came after him? After Alara, or his pups, God willing he have any?

The anxiety and indecision about what to do about that clusterfuck of a problem was something he didn't even begin to know how to tackle.

Did he mention he hated being an Alpha? If any other wolf had asked him besides Gage, he would have responded with a prompt and proud, "Hell no." Ah, shit. Who was he kidding? Even if it hadn't been Gage who'd asked him, he would have taken over leadership of the Moonstruck Pack anyway. They needed his help. He knew, despite a few soured souls, that the majority of them were honest and good people. They'd been through so much together, courtesy of Malachite. And once you'd endured hell on earth with people, you tended to be bonded for life.

The dungeons once smelled of blood, feces, and death, but now they smelled faintly like lemon. Which would have been hysterical had it not been so downright weird. He had to admit, his housekeepers did a damn good job of cleaning the place. Alara still got on to him for leaving his clothes on the floor instead of using the hamper, but seriously, what was the point when someone else was going to pick it up for him?

The girl hadn't stopped crying the entire way to the holding cells. They were nice, by prison standards, with new stone floors, clean twin beds in each cell, and a little dresser with a mirror covered in fake glass beside said beds. Clearly, his interior decorator hadn't looked up the definition of the word "dungeon" when he'd mentioned he'd wanted the place gutted and redone. Hell, it was like a damn hotel compared to what it had been during Malachite's reign.

Bastard.

He closed his eyes. *Okay, new rule—no more thinking about Malachite right now.* He had something else more pressing to deal with.

Prioritize. You're an Alpha now.

The girl sniffled as his men sat her down on a metal folding chair—with a cushion, might he add, that probably cost more than the chair was worth, thanks to the overly enthusiastic designer—and stared at her feet.

He knelt in front of her, his face a mask of apathy. "You can stop the fake waterworks now. You're not a very good actress anyway."

Almost as if on cue, her tears dried up, and she went utterly still. It was eerie as fuck. Slowly, she lifted her head and stared back at him with dead eyes. He thought "dead" because there was no emotion whatsoever within them, as if he were looking at a damn statue.

Can we say "creepy"?

He thought she might say something first or at least come back with a sarcastic quip, but her lips remained closed.

Since the endless staring was starting to creep him out, he decided to talk first. "Let's start with your name."

"I've had many."

Damn, even her voice was emotionless. Shivers broke out over his skin. "Care to elaborate?"

"I'm a doppelgänger," she said without batting a lash.

He raised a brow while resisting the urge to shudder. Doppelgängers, or skin walkers, creeped him the fuck out. All that talk about how if you saw your doppelgänger you were going to die was true. If they took your shape—your very soul, he thought, though the details were sketchy to him since he'd never actually seen a doppelgänger—then you essentially became a soulless corpse. Nik could think of few things on this earth worse than being alive and yet trapped in your own body. He'd heard stories of people murdering their own children, doing other vulgar, obscene acts, and torturing themselves if the doppelgänger required information the host was unwilling to give. But they always caved in. They had to; supposedly, the longer the doppelgänger leached off your soul, the weaker you became. He wasn't sure he'd have the kind of restraint necessary not to give in were he in that situation.

Suppressing a shiver, Nik reached out to Alara through their bond. *Call Penelope. We're going to need her help. Tell her to hurry,* he added as an afterthought.

Alara silently slipped out of the room and flipped open her cell phone just outside the door. Judging by how quickly she'd left, she was just as freaked out by their unwanted visitor as he was.

The girl's eyes darted to Alara for a second and then back to Nik's.

He growled and stepped in front of her, shielding the door from the doppelgänger's view. "You seem awfully interested in my mate."

The girl smiled. Rather than giving him the warm fuzzies, it made him want to throw up. "She's pretty."

"You mean her body is pretty."

"It's one and the same, isn't it?" she asked coyly.

Yeah. This girl was totally a wolf in sheep's clothing. "Well, you can forget about whatever it is you've come to do, because you're not going anywhere near her."

The girl grinned, her eyes sparkling with challenge. *We'll see about that,* her expression seemed to say.

He might admire her spunk if he didn't want to skewer

her.

Nik crossed his arms. Gage remained silent near the wall, surrounded by his guards. He didn't look any more pleased about this than Nik was. Nik appreciated him keeping his mouth shut and letting him handle the situation, considering he was the Alpha at Crescent Manor now and they were on Moonstruck Pack turf. Much like politics in the human world, you had to be careful about stepping on another Alpha's paws while in their den.

"Why were you in my house earlier tonight?" Nik asked. The steel in his voice warned her she better not fuck around.

She blinked, looking surprised for a split second, before her earlier arrogance returned. "I wasn't."

Nik glanced at Gage. "Do you smell bullshit?"

"I think it reeks of bullshit in here," Gage said, eyes glowing gold. "Maybe we need to try more... persuasive methods to get the answers we seek."

Nik raised a brow. Gage had never been one for torture, though Nik enjoyed the hell out of beating the shit out of bad guys. Being High King had hardened his little brother.

Good. Maybe now he'd finally be strong enough to survive the cutthroat world of Underworld politics.

"Good idea." Nik went to pick up a heavy metal object that looked as if it could be used for sawing wood.

Or bone, in this case.

The girl swallowed hard as he walked back over to her without so much as a hitch in his step. He'd done some pretty terrible things to criminals they'd tried and found guilty, but they'd always done worse. They'd deserved it.

This girl... what had she done? She couldn't help being what she was. Doppelgängers had to switch bodies in order to survive, he'd been told. The myths surrounding them were a little murky, so he didn't know exactly how they worked. But taking a saw to a girl's leg did, admittedly, make him think twice about what he was doing.

He glanced at her. Her eyes were glued to the saw, and her chest heaved as her breathing quickened. He swore she paled, though it was hard to tell with all the dirt coating her like a second skin. "Care to change your story?"

"I..." Her voice fumbled for an answer. "I'm not lying."

He shrugged. "Suit yourself. Hope you don't need this." He started to press down. The teeth of the saw bit into the grimy flesh of her thigh, drawing blood, and she yelped.

"Wait!" she shrieked. "I'll tell you!"

He almost snorted. He had no intention of actually sawing her leg off. Even he had limits. But the bluff had accomplished the desired result.

Straightening, he crossed his arms, keeping the saw in plain view as a reminder not to lie to him again. "So why are you here?"

"I..." She gulped then breathed a few deep breaths. "I sneaked in through the vents."

Shit. He made a mental note to have the whole premises swept by his warriors stat. How the hell had something like that escaped his notice? "Go on," he said.

"I came inside because I was trying to see if this was a safe place or not."

"Then you went back outside?"

She nodded, blushing. "I thought you might try to at-tack me if you caught me inside your house. If I appeared nonthreatening, outside of your home, I thought you might be more receptive to me."

"Why would you want to come here?" Gage asked.

Nik didn't mind. He'd been about to ask the same himself.

This time, the girl did drain completely of color. Her eyes were wide. She didn't look scared—she looked terrified.

"Because…" She glanced around, her voice lowering to a whisper. "I'm running from someone."

"Who?" Nik pressed when she didn't give a name.

She started to shake.

"Mistress Black."

CHAPTER FIVE

OUTSIDE THE DOOR, ALARA WENT STILL. SHE GRIPPED the cell phone she still carried after she'd gotten off a call with Penelope, the Moonstruck Pack's resident go-to White Witch. Blinking to snap out of her shock, Alara had been about to walk back inside the dungeon when she heard the girl blurt out the name that had seized control of Alara's thoughts.

Mistress Black. What the hell was the girl doing tangled up with that bitch?

Alara blinked and snapped to her senses. If the girl was running from Mistress Black, that meant she'd possibly seen her. Knew where she lived, perhaps.

If the girl had intel on the Order, Alara could use it to her advantage to find out how to destroy them.

So eager she couldn't wait, she marched into the room. "What do you know?" she demanded.

"Alara!" Nik hissed, but she growled and snapped her

teeth, which had sharpened to fangs, at him. A low snarl crept up her throat as she pinned her eyes to the terrified girl. The glow of her gaze shone pale, yellow light onto the doppelgänger's face.

"Tell me," Alara insisted, her voice scratchy, somewhere between woman and wolf. That dark desire for revenge burned hotter inside of her. She reached out and wrapped her fingers around the girl's neck, pressing her claws into her flesh. "Or I'll rip your throat out."

Nik's jaw hit the floor, as did about everyone's in the room. He stared at her a while longer before shaking his head and cautiously approaching her. "Have you lost your mind?" he said quietly. The muscle along his jaw tensed as he cast wary eyes from Alara's face to the girl's throat.

"Maybe," Alara wanted to say. The memory of her sister, her delicate body soiled in her own blood, flashed across Alara's mind. Her grip tightened. One of her claws pierced the girl's skin, drawing blood and a cry of alarm from her. "Tell me what you know. Now."

A strangled gasp slipped from the girl's mouth as Alara began to squeeze.

Alara! snapped Nik's voice in her head, loud enough to rattle her brain. And, luckily, enough to return her to her senses.

Alara blinked several times, and her grasp slackened. Her hand dropped to her side, and the girl immediately choked down a breath, grabbing at her throat. The red outline of Alara's fingers was imprinted on the girl's skin, bright against the muck, along with a thin red scratch. A dollop of fresh blood beaded on the wound, glistening.

Alara stared at those angry fingerprints and the scratch marks of her anger. She'd never lost her cool before, ever. Panic that she was losing control of herself made her body feel heavy. Order was something she'd craved. Her entire life was built upon structure, but that was one aspect of being royal she never resented. Order meant predictability, which meant safety.

Still reeling inside from what she'd done, she took a few slow steps toward the door, stumbling over the leg of a chair. "I…" Her cheeks heated. "I'm sorry."

Nik watched her without blinking, brows stooped with concern. She knew she was in for an earful of questions later.

A pale figure caught her attention from the corner of her eye, and Alara looked up to see Penelope standing in the doorway. She hadn't even heard the witch arrive. Sometimes, it frightened her how stealthy the creatures could be.

Penelope always reminded her of the Snow Queen. With her long white hair and ice-blue dress—her favorite color, it seemed, since that was the only color Alara had ever seen her wear—coupled with her sparkling snow-white complexion and blue eyes, Alara couldn't help but look at her and shiver. Penelope's personality, thankfully, was far from that of a snow queen. Warmth radiated from her, in part from how powerful Alara knew the witch to be. In the world of witches, few magical gifts were as powerful as White Magic, the power of life and light.

Nik at last tore his eyes off Alara and nodded at Penelope. "Hello, Pen. You're looking well."

Her eyes raked Nik down and back up. "Back at you."

Alara squelched the growl that started to rise in her throat. She *had* to get a grip on her anger before she did something she regretted.

Still, the wolf in her kept the White Witch on her radar as she stepped forward.

"Penelope, creepy shape-shifting asshole. Creepy shape-shifting asshole, Penelope," Nik said, gesturing between the witch and the doppelgänger. "Penelope will determine if you are what you say you are and if you're telling the truth in general." Nik crouched in front of the girl so they were eye level. She flinched, pressing her back against the chair as much as she could. "For your sake," Nik said in a low voice, "I sure as hell hope so. You don't want me to have to return."

With a gruff nod to Penelope, who watched the interaction with raised brows, Nik spun on his heel and strolled from the room. He caught Alara's wrist on the way out, pulling her along with him.

Out in the hallway, he tugged her to a stop and turned her to face him. "Care to explain what that was back there?"

"What what was?" Alara asked lightly, looking anywhere but at him. Her teeth ground together as she strained to keep her blush at bay.

"How you almost ripped a girl's throat out, for starters," Nik said in a low voice. He gazed at her intently. The worry was plainly written in the tightness of his expression.

Alara raised her chin and met his eyes. "I'll explain when you tell me what's been bothering you. You've been tense ever since the bonfire, when you first came back from your meeting with Gage."

Nik blinked and then smiled. He kissed her forehead. "Sometimes I forget I can't get anything by you. I'm not used to having people read me like a book."

She softened at the kiss, pressing a fingertip into his broad, muscular chest. "You'd better get used to it, mister. I mean, *Your Highness*."

His eyes narrowed, glittering with mischief. "Careful, love. Wouldn't want to have to punish you. You know I hate all that formality bullshit."

Alara stepped closer, pressing her breasts against him. She trailed her finger down his sternum and stomach, circling his navel before slowly proceeding south. He sucked in a gasp as her fingertip discreetly dipped below his waistline to his crotch, where the fabric was starting to tighten. "I'd say it depends on what kind of punishment you have in mind," she whispered silkily.

He growled a sigh, leaning in.

No matter how many times they touched, the warmth of his mouth always set her on fire. She closed her eyes, leaning into him as his tongue grazed hers, stroking it as his lips worked their magic in slow, savoring movements. She was stunned a little when he at last pulled away. Her eyes fluttered open, a sense of contented bewitchment making her thoughts slow.

He watched her, a slow grin lighting up his face.

Alara suppressed a smile and swatted at his arm. "Don't let it go to your head."

She started to walk back toward the dungeon to listen

to the interrogation, but Nik caught her hand. She looked at it and then at him, raising a brow.

The cocky glimmer was gone from Nik's eyes, replaced by the serious look he got when he meant business. "Not just yet, killer," he said, easing her toward the stairs.

She resisted at first, glancing over her shoulder at the dungeon and wanting so badly to hear what the doppelgänger had to say. "What if we miss something important?" *What if I miss something that could help me find the woman who ordered my family's deaths?* she thought to herself.

"If anything of immediate importance comes up, Gage has promised to notify me."

"You talked to Gage?"

He tapped his temple as they ascended the stairs. "Through the were-bond. It's especially strong between us since he's both our High King now and my brother by blood."

"Oh," was all she could think of to say. Disappointment settled on her shoulders, but she resisted the biting urge to argue. "Where are we going?"

That wicked, mischievous glint she'd grown to adore flashed across her beloved's eyes. "To do some investigating."

Penelope curiously stared at the creature in front of her. While she was a big witch and could handle herself, she couldn't help but feel more exposed to the creature since Gage, Nik, and Alara had left, Gage to call the DPI and check on his mate, the worrywart, and Alara and Nik, who the hell knew? Danica must have been too freaked out to come inside the dungeon. Penelope had spoken with her in the hall when she'd first arrived, where the were queen was waiting patiently for her mate. Penelope couldn't blame Danica—the doppelgänger made her whole body rigid with tension.

She'd heard of doppelgängers, of course. Had she seen one? No, even being as old as she was. White Witches often lived extended lives thanks to their regenerative powers. She'd thought she'd encountered every manner of strange creature in the Underworld, but this one down-right fascinated her.

The girl stared back at her without blinking, a slight smile on her face. It was unnerving, like a wax doll's smile. Those damn things had always creeped her out.

Snap out of it. Act like the professional you are.

Summoning a camera from thin air with a pop and a flash of white light, she muttered a levitation spell. The object hovered in the air, suspended in front of the dungeon, its lens aimed at the doppelgänger and Penelope. With a flick of her wrist, Penelope had it recording.

She cleared her throat and walked around the girl, circling her once. "What is your name?"

A grin. "Which one?"

Penelope raised a brow, stopping in front of the girl and crossing her arms. "You think this is a game? That the wolves won't kill you?"

"Doesn't matter. I can always find a new body." She looked Penelope over as she said it.

A chill crawled up Penelope's spine. She had the sense the creature in front of her wasn't exactly evil, but it wasn't entirely good, either. It simply… was. It did what it needed to in order to survive.

Even if that meant invading someone else's body.

"What's the matter?"

Penelope blinked, startled out of her thoughts. "Excuse me?"

"You look pale," the girl said in that eerie monotone voice of hers. "Do I unsettle you?"

That's an understatement. More like scare the shit out of me. The urge to get the hell out of there as quickly as possible took over. Swallowing hard, she said, "Close your eyes."

"Why?"

Penelope pursed her lips. "I need to scan you."

"You can try." Another cunning smile.

Oh, so you want to play games, huh?

Penelope looked at the two guards standing watch just inside the room, by the door. "You may wish to step out. I can handle this."

They looked at each other, not moving.

Penelope growled a sigh. "The extraction spell I'm about to perform may have… unpleasant side effects on anyone else in the room." When they still didn't move, she elaborated. "Vomiting, diarrhea, reliving every painful, horrible memory you've ever had, for starters. Oh, and let's not forget there is the slight chance you could get stuck in one of your memories, good or bad. The spell makes no distinction."

That got their attention. One guard started out the door, but the other paused. "Wait. Our liege said—"

"Nik entrusted me with getting the information he needed. And as I don't see him or Alara, or the High King or Queen, around, that means I'm in charge. Now, get out. Last warning." The sooner she could be done with this, the better. The creature made her skin crawl.

With a "hmph," she turned and raised her arms, palms facing outward toward the bound doppelgänger. She heard a door close and felt the wolves' presence leave the room as her fingertips began to shine with sparkling white light.

A low, melodic hum filled the room, as if hundreds of sets of fingers were sliding along the rims of half-filled wineglasses. Strings of light slowly glided from her fingers as she chanted in an old language long forgotten. As the threads grew longer, they branched out, their shimmering fingers reaching for the doppelgänger.

The girl stared at the strands, not flinching as they seeped inside her head and into the darkest recesses of her memory.

Now, let's find out your secrets.

The spell always took a few minutes to settle, for the prongs to find their places. The spell had to move slowly so as not to damage the brain. One wrong move, and someone could be brain dead.

It felt as if an eternity passed. All the while, the doppelgänger remained still, staring back at Penelope with dull eyes. Her whole expression was completely lifeless. Penelope resisted the urge to work faster.

When she came into her powers, she took an oath

to never harm anyone without just cause. So far, the girl hadn't done anything more than freak her out. She couldn't help what she was, just as Penelope couldn't help being a witch.

At long last, she felt the magic find its bearings and settle. With all the care of a surgeon, Penelope began to pull back on the strings, to extract whatever information the doppelgänger guarded. But it wouldn't come. It was as if the memories were snagged on something.

What?

She tugged again, applying a little more pressure. No, she was sure of it. The memories really were stuck.

"What the hell?" she breathed. In all her life, she'd never encountered anything like this. Sure, some people were excellent at guarding their thoughts, making the memories feel as if they were being pulled from mud, but Penelope was always able to wrench them free. She had never failed, and for the first time in her life, she was afraid she might not succeed.

Warning bells went off in her head. Honestly, she was probably freaking out over nothing. Doppelgängers inhabited other people's bodies—thusly, there shouldn't be anything odd about their brains. At least, that's what her spellbooks said.

Knowing she just needed to tug a little harder, Penelope braced herself and gave a stronger pull.

This time, something tugged *back.*

She gasped, stumbling forward slightly. Her brain reeled as her heart hammered inside her chest. Had she imagined that? She had to have. No one, not even the most iron-willed witch or warlock, was capable of controlling the extraction threads embedded in their brains. Not only would it be incredibly painful, but it could also cause irreparable harm to the patient. Convinced she was only paranoid and had imagined things, Penelope took a deep breath to steady her nerves and tried pulling again.

This time, something yanked her forward so violently that her face nearly slammed into the dungeon's bars. Spooked, she jerked the threads back, but her magic wouldn't come. Penelope's heartbeat kicked up several notches as she bordered on hysteria. "What the...?" she gasped. Her magic thrashed against whatever it was caught on, but that only caused whatever had hold of her to pull harder. She winced, struggling to break free as the magic was leeched from her. All witches' magic was rooted deep within their souls, the source of their power. It felt as if her veins were lighting on fire. A cry of pain slipped out, and she promptly bit her tongue. Her feet slid along the ground. She dug in her heels, the soles of her shoes squeaking along the floor as she was dragged forward, toward the girl.

A sharp pain started in her chest, and she exhaled violently. It felt as though someone had driven a needle straight into her heart, and it had splintered inside of her. With every pulse, the pinpricks of pain intensified, spreading along her arms and legs. Her veins glowed bright white in her arms. The light gushed from her fingertips in a torrent of magic. Oh God, she could actually *see* the magic drain from her body.

No, not her magic—her *soul*.

Futilely, she tried calling it back, but she was so sleepy and weak now. Her eyelids drooped, causing the hot tears gathered in the rims of her eyes to spill onto her cheeks.

A quiet, dark laugh chilled the air.

Penelope's watery eyes widened.

The doppelgänger's eyes were black. She smiled. "Finally," spoke a different voice, this one much older sounding. "Someone useful."

Penelope's face paled as she shrank away in fear, at least as far as the threads that bound her to that nightmare would let her. "Who are you?" she rasped.

The doppelgänger's eyes glowed purple. "I am death."

The strings of light attached to the doppelgänger's head slowly began to turn black, as if dipped in ink. Penelope nearly gagged on the stench and raw power of—

She gasped. *Black Magic.*

She was suffocating. *Oh, help!* She couldn't breathe! "What… are… you… doing?" she choked out, but the last of her breath was sucked from her as the ink found the other end of the lines and poured itself into her veins.

It burned. Oh merciful God, it stung. The Black Magic seared her blood, spreading quicker and quicker until it felt as if her whole body was aflame.

Through the blinding pain, she thought she screamed, but she couldn't be sure. Everything was so, so quiet.

And then, blissfully, mercifully, everything was black.

CHAPTER SIX

LARA NEVER GOT TIRED OF GAZING AT THE MOON. AS A child, she'd sit in her mother's garden, curled up comfortably on a plush blanket in the grass, while she watched the night age.

Like most werewolves, her senses came alive at night. Though heightened at all times, the dark of the night had a way of pulling forward her inner wolf, calling upon its strengths while subduing the physical weaknesses of her human side. For as proper as she'd been brought up, she never felt restricted or guarded at night. No, at night, she could be herself.

She could be free.

Nik didn't let go of her hand as they slipped into the woods ringing the manor's vast, immaculately mowed lawn. His pulse thrummed through her; she could feel his heartbeat pumping in rhythm with her own. The mate-bond was funny like that. It was eerie at first, maybe even a little invasive, having someone else's presence constantly in her head. But the more she grew accustomed to him, the more she knew she could never go back to being totally by herself. The thought sent a lonely chill through her.

A myriad of smells assaulted her senses as their footsteps stirred up dirt and leaves: the damp, musty smell of the earth, the sweet scent of moss, and the more subdued smell of bark. Animal smells—deer, raccoons, birds—swirled in and out of the other scents. Sometimes it was a chore to untangle everything.

The DPI will be here soon, Nik said through their mate-bond, the sound of his deep, slightly raspy voice reverberating inside her head. *I want another look around the area before they show up and block it off and their scents start muddying things up.*

Makes sense. And you brought me because…?

The serious expression he'd worn since they left the house turned into a grin. *Your nose is keener than mine, love. Not to mention I wanted to spend time alone with my mate.*

So you wanted to get me alone. In the woods. Not creepy at all.

You know you're excited.

The hunger inside her stirred as heat tickled her tummy. "Excited" didn't begin to cover it.

It didn't take long to get to the spot where they'd found the doppelgänger. Or rather, where the doppelgänger had found them.

The scent of their lovemaking still hung in the air, though it wasn't nearly as pronounced as it had been earlier.

Should we shift? Alara asked, eyeing her mate with a raised brow. Moonlight and shadows dappled his face while lighting up their surroundings with varying shades of gray. A few fireflies clung to the tree canopy above, their dainty yellow lights twinkling. Crickets chirped in a soft hum, and in the distance, she heard a brook laughing. It was peaceful, soothing. She could easily stay out here all night, using nothing but the grass and soil for a bed.

Nik nodded. *Ladies first.*

A thrill of anticipation ratcheted through her. Hardly able to wait, she closed her eyes and released the wolf within. With a snarl, it barreled to the surface. Her bones morphed, her skin stretching to accommodate the Change. While uncomfortable—because let's be honest, who can say they enjoy having all their bones basically broken and rebuilt?—it was nothing compared to the pain she'd endured with gritted teeth and steel-willed determination during her first Change. *That* had been downright brutal.

The transformation was over in less than a few seconds, and two majestic, large brown wolves stood there.

The scent of the doppelgänger immediately slammed into her nose. *God*, it was sour, like rotting flesh and rotten eggs and roadkill in July.

Alara whined, and Nik barked his agreement. She immediately shifted all of her focus to the task at hand and began sniffing around the ground. The sooner they could get this investigation rolling, the sooner she could try to forget this ungodly stench.

It wasn't hard to pick out the doppelgänger's odor

from the myriad of other smells. Even though Nick had said her nose was keener, she doubted he'd have needed her help tracking this scent. It was like that person who wore a summer color, like neon pink, to a funeral; they stood out no matter what.

With a bark to follow her, Alara tore off through the woods.

She never tired of running in her wolf's body, of the power of her muscles, the clarity of her senses, and the surety in her step. In this form, she never had to worry about being too fat, too curvy, too pale, too quiet, or any other bullshit insecurities. When she Changed, the instinct of a predator took over, and all her worries and fears melted away.

If only she could stay a wolf.

Nik was close behind, his powerful strides sending reverberations through the ground and up into her own legs. The cool night air kissed her face, whipping her fur back as the world raced by.

So free, so fast.

Elation filled her, and she barked out the wolf equivalent of a laugh. For the first time in weeks, she meant it and could feel the joy. Anytime she laughed or smiled, it felt forced. Fake, somehow.

But with the night all around, and no human worries pressing on her shoulders, she finally felt the pressure, agony, and suffering lift. It was the lightest she'd felt in weeks.

Nik barked right back, weaving in and out of her path in a silly zigzag pattern.

You're going to get hurt, she chided gently.

Nah. I'm an Alpha.

What does that have to do with mashing your maw in on a tree?

Everything. It automatically means I'm a badass, equipped with grace, agility—holy shit!

Alara nearly died laughing as he came within an inch of slamming mouth first into a low-hanging branch. He'd leapt over a log, not seeing the branch until it was nearly too late, thanks to the shadows and him not paying attention.

You think that's funny, huh? he said wryly. He nipped her on the rear, and she rushed to tag him back, turning it into a game as they tracked. After about a mile of running, another smell hit Alara's nose, just as acrid as the doppelgänger's and yet bitterer, like charred flesh. Alara barely registered that it was strange, she was so taken with the chase. The drug of freedom, laughter, and play was intoxicating, and she started to lose focus.

Screw duty and honor. She was having fun, dammit.

The tree line broke, and they spilled out into an open meadow surrounding a small lake. Nik had taken her here a few times, bringing along picnic baskets and food he'd grilled himself in one of his surprisingly sweet moments. Since coming back to Crescent Manor, Alara had discovered Nik was obsessed with his crappy little thirty-dollar grill from Wal-Mart. She'd offered to get him a more sophisticated one, but he'd said he liked that one. "It's unassuming, doesn't put on any airs, and gets the job done right," he'd said, grinning. "Just like me."

Alara never understood the bond between men and

inanimate objects. Cars, grills, video game consoles… Her father hadn't been immune, either. It was a well-known fact that the High King enjoyed playing Xbox late at night to take his mind off things.

A rush of longing to see him again, along with a jolt of bitterness for his betrayal, wracked her core. No matter how hot her hatred burned, she couldn't seem to erase the small part of her that still loved and missed her father. Which only pissed her off more. It would be so much easier to just hate him.

With a growl and renewed energy fueled by anger, she started toward the woods on the opposite side of the meadow, but Nik called out *Hey, hold up for a second.*

Alara obeyed, though nervous energy made her paw at the earth. *Is something wrong?* she said after a moment of silence, unable to hide her impatience. Her unresolved feelings for her father were once again on her mind, making her feel confused, hurt, and angry. The sooner she could distract herself, with, let's say, tracking, the sooner she could dismiss those troublesome feelings she had no desire to figure out.

In a blink and a flash of light, Nik Shifted back to his human form. Moonlight painted the contours of his hard muscles in silver, the shadows accentuating every curve and valley. The intricate, swirling filigree of their mating tattoos ran over his shoulders and chest down to his pectorals. The ink glittered with deep-blue crystals. It was mesmerizing.

Change, he said through their mate-bond. No, not said—commanded.

The heat of lust filtered through their bond, making Alara ache deep within. Her eyes fluttered down her mate's gorgeous body to his proud erection, crowned in moonlight.

Oh.

Well, she'd wanted a distraction. And if she had a choice, hot werewolf sex under the open sky by a beautiful lake would be at the top of her list.

In no time at all, Alara Shifted back to herself, her human skin snapping into place like a spandex glove. Her skin felt feverish, her chest rising and falling rapidly as she caught her breath.

Her mate held her gaze, his eyes still taking on the wolfish glow. Without a word, he stalked toward her, all raw muscle and power. As he buried one hand in her hair and pressed the other against the small of her back, his mouth claimed hers, snatching away the breath she'd sought.

She groaned as he deepened the kiss, drawing her more tightly to him. His hot tongue slid along hers, filling her mouth with his taste.

It was a wolf thing, she knew. The desire to claim, to mark one's territory. The leash around her more carnal nature always loosened whenever she switched forms. And usually the best way to cage the beast, so to speak, was with hot and furious sex. Or a cold shower. But which one was more appealing?

Nik's hands roved her body, feeling her curves, the calluses along his palms sending shivers cascading across her body and leaving trails of fire in their wake. The crown of his sex rubbed hers, seeking entrance to the hot dampness between her legs. Her own sex began to throb with need. She reached down and grabbed his hardened cock, positioning it so it might more easily slide in.

Nik growled with approval and then chuckled. "Impatient, are we?"

"Have you met me?" she said with a breathless smile.

Nik answered with another hungry kiss. Picking her up, he gently laid her on the grass, nudging her legs open with his knees. His cock brushed her sex, and she raised her hips to meet his as he thrust into her, fully cloaking himself in her.

She moaned as liquid pleasure coursed through her veins as he began to pump furiously, bucking her hips against his as he had her.

He lowered his torso over her, one hand gripping her head and the other behind her back, pressing upward so her hips would remain raised. She scored his back with her nails as he thrust harder, faster. The first quake of coming undone blossomed deep within her belly. In an explosion of color and light, she came as a moan tore from her throat and she arched her back.

A moment later, he groaned hard in his throat, his hot liquid pouring into her and warming her from the inside out.

As she came down off the high of her climax, she inhaled deeply, staring into the night sky over his heaving shoulders. She could feel the tension drain from her body, her muscles becoming languid.

God, she'd needed this. They both had, a release from

the mounting pressures of ruling a pack of wolves and try-ing to keep the rest of the paranormal world from falling apart.

They lay there, coated in sweat, the sweetness of their lovemaking clinging to their pores and making Alara lightheaded with joy. Then again, maybe that was her af-terglow following that earth-shattering orgasm.

Nik gently played with her hair, twining it around his finger and letting it loose before starting again. The breeze shifted, bringing with it the crispness of the water. You wouldn't think water would have a smell, but Alara could always tell where a stream, brook, or lake was. Water had a mineral tang to it, like how a wet cave smelled.

"What are you thinking about?" Nik murmured.

Stretching, she nestled closer to him and smiled as she gazed up into his face. "About how water smells."

"Water has a smell?"

She nodded.

"I'll take your word for it. Half the time, I can't smell shit, thanks to all this pollen and dust."

"Perhaps we should take a vacation once this is all over. Give your sinuses a break."

"Eh. I'd probably find something to be allergic to wherever we went."

True. Nik was allergic to everything: dust, hay, cats. He was even mildly allergic to dog dander, including that of werewolves, ironically enough. She wasn't sure if her nose was just keener because her sense of smell really was sharper than the average werewolf's or if her sense of smell was sharper simply because Nik's sucked so much.

"I was also thinking about what a fantastic lover you are," Alara said, petting his chest hair. He was about right for her tastes; not furry enough to qualify as a Chia Pet, but having just enough hair to be masculine.

Nik's grin returned. "Don't you forget it."

She smacked his chest lightly. "You're supposed to say, 'My skills are nothing compared to yours, Alara.'"

"I won't dispute that." The low rumble in his voice, combined with the flash of gold in his eyes, made her inner wolf whine to rut again.

The desire in her mate's expression flickered, interrupted by that same doubt and troubled gaze she'd seen earlier at the bonfire. "What is it?" she asked softly.

He knew better than to try to hide something from her. For one, it was nearly impossible with the mate-bond. Even if you were perfectly poker faced, your emotions would ultimately betray you.

Swallowing heavily, Nik spilled what Gage had told him in the office about Malachite and his quest for revenge against the Moonstruck Pack.

Alara grew still, not even daring to breathe as he finished. Heavy silence hung in the air.

She blinked, swallowed, then blinked again, trying to make sense of it. While the wolves under her rule weren't exactly saints, they'd never struck her as cold-hearted killers. Then again, what did she know about them? She'd only been here a few weeks.

"What do you think?" he asked at last.

She took in a deep breath and sighed, shaking her head in disbelief. "It's…"

"Hard to believe?"

"Yeah. For starters. What are you going to do?"

"I don't know yet." He leaned his head back, staring up at the stars with a hard expression. "If it's all true, I honestly can't say I blame Malachite. Speaking from experience, I can relate to how angry he was. I couldn't guarantee I wouldn't do the same thing. It's natural to want to make someone suffer for hurting those you love."

A sentiment Alara also found relatable.

"I would want justice," Nick went on. "I do want justice. But I'm going to have to do some investigating to see what really happened. Malachite was also an impulsive liar. He could have been bullshitting us just to stir up trouble."

Judging from what she'd heard of the legendary Alpha, she didn't think it sounded unreasonable.

"We'll figure it out." She hugged her mate, pressing her cheek against his strong chest. "Whatever comes, we'll face it together. I'll support you, no matter what you decide to do. But, for what it's worth, I believe we should find out whether we share our house with cutthroats and child murderers. And if so, punish them according to the Laws of the Underworld and banish them."

"Agreed." He took the hand she had rested on his chest, bringing it to his mouth to press a kiss along her knuckles.

Tension still radiated through their bond. "Anything else on your mind?" she asked.

Nik's lips pressed together. "I'm scared." He chuckled bitterly. "I'm actually fucking scared to move forward."

She didn't need to ask why. She already knew.

"The pack is in danger of falling apart as it is," Nik said. "If I start sniffing around in the past and digging up their skeletons, I may start a mutiny. Gage couldn't have picked a worse fucking time to deliver this news."

"Would you rather he'd kept quiet?"

"No," he answered honestly. "Still doesn't mean it doesn't suck."

Alara rubbed his arm reassuringly. "You're strong. And smart and clever and a lot of other things that make up a good Alpha. We'll be fine. The pack will be fine, and once this is all over, we'll all be stronger for it."

In the moment of reflective silence that followed, a question jumped to her mind that she couldn't resist asking. "What do you think will happen to the doppelgänger?"

He returned her hand to his chest and soothingly rubbed it with his thumb. "Not sure," he admitted. "But I promise you, we won't stop looking for Mistress Black. We'll get justice for your family."

Her eyes narrowed. "I want her dead. I want to kill her myself."

His thumb paused. A moment later, he sat up, propping his head up on one elbow to look at her. "I urge you to reconsider. Let me finish," he said, holding up a hand as she was about to interrupt. "Killing changes you. It blackens your soul, and once you cross that line, you can never turn back. You're too pure, Alara. I don't want your soul stained, like mine is. I've killed before. I've watched the life drain from my enemies' eyes. And I always wondered later... who were they? Did they have families? Children? A lover who will never see them again?"

"I don't care," Alara said darkly, her anger taking over. "I want her dead."

"I know." Nik cupped her face, the roughness of his palms prickling against her skin. "And I promise you, you'll have your revenge. But don't sacrifice who you are as a person to get it."

What other way was there? Wait around for someone else to kill Mistress Black? Or worse, wait for the DPI to take her into custody to give her "a fair trial," sentence her to life in prison, dump her in a private cell, and forget about her for the next however many years while she painted her toenails in prison?

There was also the chilling possibility of a politician getting hold of her. A powerful and rare Black Witch, with a network of willing followers, could come in handy. There were elections to be won, profits to be made by any means necessary...

Alara knew the aristocracy of the Underworld, and what she did know made her shudder. She could think of several bitches and pricks who wouldn't bat a lash to kiss Mistress Black's ass if it meant getting ahead—regardless of her atrocities.

On the verge of arguing, Alara opened her mouth— and all the air rushed right back out of her.

Nik's eyes were so earnest, the hope that he was somehow saving her soul shining through.

Her heart cracked.

She couldn't do it. No way could she bear to tell him that he was wasting his breath.

That her soul had been damned the moment she'd laid

eyes on her sister's bleeding corpse.

Forcing her lips together into a tight smile, she nodded once and looked away. He cupped her chin and gently turned her head back to face him.

"Promise me you won't do anything reckless or crazy?" he said.

The thought of her doing something reckless or crazy would have been laughable a few weeks ago. Now… now it seemed more likely with each passing day.

"I can't make a promise I don't know I'll be able to keep," she said carefully. She pressed her lips to his palm. "But I shall try."

"That's all I can ask for." He kissed her forehead and pulled her in close, wrapping his strong arms around her and holding her tight. "I don't want to lose you."

She hugged him, pressing her ear against his chest so she could listen to the beating of his heart. "You won't. Not in this lifetime or the next. Not if I can ever help it."

He rested his head against hers, sighing contentedly. "I love you."

She startled. She'd felt his love, sure. She was positive she had. But until now, he'd never actually said the words that meant the world to her.

Lifting her head, she looked up into his eyes, searching them. No joke there.

She couldn't recall hearing those words from her parents' mouths. From her sister, Izzy's, yes, but never from theirs. Not that she could remember, anyway.

Warm tears stung her eyes, and she looked down at his chest. "I love you too," she whispered, as if saying it too loudly meant placing a target on his back for the bad guys. It seemed whenever she loved something—her sister, college classes, you name it—it got taken away. As if her love was cursed. Which was silly. Life just happened—that she knew. But the bad stuff always seemed to happen to her, and that kind of run-of-the-mill, continuous bad luck made you wary as hell.

A growl of desire rumbled in Nik's chest, and his eyes glistened with golden light. He was growing hard again, which only served to fuel her own mounting fire.

"We should either finish our tracking or get back," she said roughly, her throat dry.

"We have plenty of time to track. And they won't miss us for five more minutes." His head leaned in as he angled his mouth for hers.

The wind shifted directions again, this time bringing with it the charred scent Alara had detected—and dismissed—earlier. Nik's spine straightened, and in response, she went tense in his arms. "What is that?"

"Don't know," he said grimly. "But I think it may be human."

Getting up and Changing again to follow the scent was harder than Alara had anticipated. Lying there alone with her mate, hidden away in the forest from the outside world and its troubles, was like dying and going to Heaven. It didn't get much better than that.

She envied Danica and Gage their honeymoon. Werewolves didn't believe in traditional weddings, but Alara could certainly appreciate the romantic side of it. While the mating ceremony was enough for her, a lovers' getaway sounded fantastic right about now.

No witches.

No bitterness, no grief.

Okay, well, those last two things would probably still be there. Wounds from death took a while to heal, possibly years. She was just so ready to stop hurting all the time that she would almost pay any price to escape the agony.

This time Nik took the lead, tearing through the underbrush with scarcely a sound. A living, breathing shadow of death.

Alara charged after him, her own footfalls light and graceful. It had taken a while to trust this other form, but now she surrendered to it completely. It had never steered her wrong, these senses that were so much more attuned to the world, these muscles, teeth, and claws that made her feel invincible.

The charred scent took them up the river and into a small hollow where the ground had sunk beneath a tree. Exposed roots tangled along the ground, some thick, some small.

Something white stuck out of the soil just below the embankment. Nik leapt, seizing the white object in his mouth before pulling. Whatever it was didn't want to come loose easily. It took a few tugs, along with Alara pawing at the earth to thin it, before the object dislodged itself and tumbled to the ground.

Alara's eyes focused on it—and terror jolted her out of wolf form so abruptly that she had to clap a hand over her mouth to keep from screaming.

CHAPTER SEVEN

OLY FUCK, THIS THING *STANK*. SMELLING IT WAS THE
equivalent to being slapped in the face, kicked in the
balls, and then run over by a bus.

For the first time ever, Nik was actually eager to change
back into a human. Maybe his "inferior" senses would be
enough to subdue the smell.

No such luck.

There was no escaping it—it was that bad, even as a
human. Or maybe his olfactory organs had shriveled up
and locked the noxious gases inside his nose. "Damn," he
rasped. Too late, he realized he'd used his breath up and
would have to inhale the rotten stench. If he were a kid, he
might have even thrown a temper tantrum, complete with
unholy wailing and a kicking fit.

The smell of putrid flesh singed his throat, making
him gag.

About that time, a memory popped into his head.

The pack kept several community refrigerators in the two kitchens within the manor. Now, a pack of unruly werewolves who weren't exactly well known for great personal hygiene weren't the best at keeping things neat and tidy. Food often got banished to the recesses of the fridges, forgotten about until some poor soul stumbled upon it while trying to find their sandwich meat. Nik had been one such soul. In an irritating attempt at locating the pepper jack cheese he'd recently bought, he'd nearly torn the fridge apart and had stumbled upon a seemingly innocent plastic container.

No name scribbled on the lid in Sharpie. No clue as to what it contained.

Nik should have known better. He really should have. Opening up the lid before he could think otherwise, he'd been assaulted by the most rank-ass piece of rotting steak he'd ever smelled. He'd never forgotten that smell, the sickly sweet-yet-sourness of it.

This corpse reminded him of that. Including its ability to coat his tongue every time he took a breath, giving him a taste of it.

Alara looked green. Her cheeks kept puffing out, as if she were trying to keep from throwing up.

They both needed to get the fuck out of there before the damned thing caused them to pass out. And wouldn't that just look cute when the DPI showed up? The two of them, buck naked, out cold beside a dead body.

No, that wouldn't be suspicious at aaaalllllll.

The soil must have been masking the stench, Nik said through their bond, opting for it so he didn't taste that thing's odor any more than he had to. Someone had gone to a lot of trouble to hide this. Not well enough, apparently. Judging by the chewed-up skin around the elbow that was poking out of the earth, he knew that the animals had found it and begun to do their thing.

God, can we bury it again?

His sentiments exactly. *We'll get out of here soon. I promise.* Nik knelt, his knees barely touching the soft earth.

It was a woman. At least, he thought those shriveled lumps on top of the person's chest had once been breasts. The entire body was sunk in on itself, as if someone—or something—had literally sucked all the juices from it.

Ew.

Alara knelt beside him, her eyes showing confusion as they swept across the corpse. *What happened to it?*

Don't know, Nik said grimly, standing. *But I'd wager our doppelgänger friend is involved.*

He didn't know if they were capable of this, but it seemed likely. He couldn't think of anything else that would do this to a victim.

The skin wasn't rotted, either. Pale and cracked as shit but not falling off the bone. Meaning it hadn't been there long, maybe a day or two.

Just how long had that damned creepy-ass monster been lurking in the woods? And more importantly, why the hell hadn't he sensed it?

God, you suck as an Alpha went through his mind before he firmly shut that thought down. Yes, he'd been distracted. Wondering if his pack was going to go all Caesar on him made him that way. With the impending uprising, Gage's arrival, and worrying about his grieving mate, his brain hadn't had much room for thinking about anything else.

Still, he should have known something was up. The doppelgänger's smell was like a glowing neon sign, it was that strong.

So why hadn't any of his border patrols picked up on it?

Hey, look.

Nik walked around to the other side of the corpse, where Alara knelt. She pointed to the dirt about a foot away.

Nik frowned, inching closer. It looked as if someone, most likely the victim here, had scribbled something into the dirt. The crude image was smudged, as if the body had been dragged partially through it. It looked as if the victim had tried to spell something out before she'd met her demise.

The heat from Alara's body warmed the chill at his back as she crouched beside him and drew her finger in the air over the letters. E-Y-E-S.

Eyes? Nik said. *What the hell does that have to do with anything?*

I'm not sure. There must be a clear reason why she wrote it. Otherwise, why bother?

True. That was a puzzle they'd have to solve later. By now, they had so many pieces Nik wasn't sure how to fit them all together.

We should be getting back, Nik said, rising. *I can hear*

sirens about three miles out.

I hear them too. Together, they both Shifted, running as fast and far away from the corpse as their paws would take them.

Nik greedily gulped down large mouthfuls of air, eager to purge his body of the nasty smell clinging to his nostrils. *That was some epic stink. I don't think I'll ever get that smell out of my system.*

Me either. I feel like it's clinging to my pores.

That made two of them. It was like a slimy sheen of sweat.

Are we going to tell the DPI about the corpse? Alara asked.

We'll have to. They'll smell us out there. I'll tell them we did a perimeter check. They won't be too happy about it, but I'll push the fact that it's my land, I'm the Alpha, and thus, in charge of my pack's well-being, including guests. I'm not taking any chances, especially not with the High King and Queen here.

Nik hated working with the DPI bastards. Yeah, sure, there were a few good cops, but there were far too many corrupt and incompetent ones in the region's department for his liking.

Verika would have whipped them into shape.

That thought jarred him. It used to feel natural to associate Verika's name with the DPI. Used to hurt like hell too when Nik and Verika had split. Now... now it was just an extra thought, without any kind of emotion, good or bad, tied to it. That realization lifted an enormous amount of weight from Nik's wolf shoulders.

Finally, fucking finally. He was over Verika.

Alara restrained a whine as a branch cut her cheek.

Nik glanced at her sharply. Alara never ran into things, especially not as a wolf. *What's wrong?*

You still think about her. Don't you?

It took Nik a moment to realize whom she was talking about. *Oh shit.* Had he thought about Verika out loud, through their bond? It wasn't the first time something like this had happened, albeit it'd never been about ex-girlfriends, thank God.

Alara—

It's fine. I understand. Her brusque tone suggested she didn't.

It's not like that, Nik insisted. Alara tended to clam up on topics she didn't want to talk about. Not that he was one to judge. He was the exact same way. But he couldn't let her stew on this, as he knew she would, not while they had more pressing matters to deal with, and he needed her to be on the same page as him.

Nik, you don't have to explain yourself, Alara said tiredly. The hint of sadness in her voice threatened to crack his heart in two. *She was your first true love. I get it. Those people are impossible to forget.*

You've got it all wrong, he growled. *Despite what it may look like—*

Nik, Alara, clipped Gage's voice in their heads. *You need to get back here stat.*

What's happened? Nik asked, instantly in business mode.

It's Penelope. Something happened to her while she was

interrogating the doppelgänger.

Nik swore. *We're on our way.*

Not another word was said about Verika, or anything else for that matter. The topic of an ex-girlfriend, he knew, was so trivial considering this most recent development that it wasn't even worth bringing up at this time.

And all the while they ran, he couldn't help but feeling that this was just the calm before the storm.

They were both exhausted by the time they got back. Their legs like Jell-O, they Shifted and stumbled up the stairs and through the door just off the main floor's kitchen. The cook was cleaning up. She looked up, took a gander at them, and without a word retrieved some clothes from the closet in the corner of the room. It might seem weird to humans, but werewolves tended to keep clothing stored in every room. After all, you never knew when you might need a fresh change of clothes, having shredded your last garments while Changing into a furry killing machine.

Gage met them outside the dungeon. *Find anything?* he asked Nik.

Yeah. We'll discuss it later. What's going on? He followed his brother into the dungeon. Penelope was sitting in a chair, clutching at her head and looking paler than she usually did. Her normally impeccably styled hair was disheveled, and her clothing looked torn in places. Nik's frown deepened as his eyes went from her to the doppelgänger slumped over in the chair just inside a closed cell.

"Pen says she was in the middle of a spell when it

backfired, knocking the doppelgänger and her out," Gage said. He cast another worried glance at the White Witch, lowering his voice. "We can't get much else out of her. She says she's having a hard time remembering what happened, an apparent side effect of spells gone bad."

"Where are the other witnesses?"

Gage sighed. "The guards weren't there."

Nik blinked, trying to process this idiocy. "*What?*" he growled.

"Hold on, there," Gage said, holding up a hand. "They said Penelope asked them to step out, saying she didn't want to endanger them. Apparently the spell she worked was no simple feat."

"Nik!"

They both looked up as Penelope stumbled toward him, to the disgruntlement of the resident werewolf doctor seeing to her. Penelope's pale, thin fingers clasped the sleeves of Nik's shirt. "I'm so sorry," she blurted, staring up into his eyes. "I couldn't hold it…"

"Just calm down, Penelope," Nik said, grasping hold of her shoulders. She was shaking like a leaf. Nik couldn't recall a time he'd ever seen the woman rattled. She hadn't even so much as blinked while facing down a swarm of wraiths. "Just tell me what happened. Do you remember anything?"

Alara listened silently behind him as Penelope nodded, a mixture of pain and confusion washing over her face.

"Some of it, yes," Penelope said. "I was working on the girl, an extraction spell, right after I asked the guards to leave. Something… blackness…" Her eyelids started to flutter shut, and Nik caught her as her body went limp.

"Pen? Pen!" He shook her slightly, but she had passed out. "Damn," he swore after handing her off to the doctor. "I've never heard of a spell backfiring on Pen. Have you?"

Gage shook his head. "All magic is risky, especially that which penetrates the mind."

Alara shivered, hugging herself.

"It's possible it didn't go as planned because the doppelgänger has warped the way this girl's brain works," Gage finished.

Chills popped up along Nik's arms as he stared at the girl. Was that what doppelgängers did? Got inside you and screwed up your internal wiring? Would you even know who you were anymore if the doppelgänger left? Would you have any memories of anyone or anything dear to you, any sense of self?

The thought of forgetting who he was, of being shut out from accessing his own body, made him queasy.

One of the guards Nik had ordered to guard Penelope walked in right about then.

Nik immediately rounded on him, nerves and lack of sleep making his fuse much too short. Before the guard could blink, Nik had grabbed a handful of his shirt and slammed him against the prison wall.

"Nik," Alara said with warning, placing a hand on his arm.

"What the hell happened?" Nik barked.

The guard's eyes were wide. Clearly, he hadn't expected to be assaulted as soon as he came in the room. "I—I don't know. Penelope ordered us out. Everything was silent for about twenty minutes."

"And then what?"

He gulped, paling as his frightened eyes shifted to Penelope. "Then we heard her screaming, a God-awful sound, like the hounds of hell were after her," he said quietly.

The fuck? What the hell happened to you, Pen?

Alara squeezed his arm again, this time digging in her nails. *Nik,* she said in his head.

His anger having been replaced by fear and a little paranoia, he slowly let go of the were's shirt. "Sorry, Alex," Nik murmured. "I'm a little tense."

"It's-It's fine," Alex stuttered. Words tumbled out of his mouth. "Actually, I came to tell you that the DPI is here."

Great. Just one more headache to deal with.

"Thank you," Nik said with a curt nod. "Show them in. The sooner we can get this doppelgänger out of here, the better."

If Alara protested, she didn't say so. She nibbled on her lip, a sexy little habit she always did while mulling over something. He'd have to gather her thoughts on the matter later.

Alex pressed his fist across his chest and bowed before leaving.

Nik felt his neck muscles draw tight, the low throb along the back of his head heralding a tension headache. Funny how the DPI could always trigger one.

Upstairs, the front door creaked open. He knew it was the front entrance because of the loose groan the wood gave whenever it moved, like an old man grumbling about being disturbed. Several footsteps walked across the foyer, heading in their direction.

"I'll go meet them," Gage said. Gently, he touched Alara's and Nik's elbows, drawing their attention to him. *There was one more thing Verika told me,* Gage said to both of them through their telepathic werewolf links. *The DPI has been compromised. Some of them are working for Mistress Black, but we don't know who.*

A jolt of panic went up from Alara, and Nik rolled his eyes, suppressing a groan. *You have got to be kidding me,* he said. *And you're just telling us now, as they're "storming the castle"?*

I know, I know. I forgot earlier because I was so wrapped up in telling you about Malachite, then we ran out of time before the party began.

This was important, dammit. He would have pushed back the party, maybe even canceled it, to learn this awesome little development.

"Look, I've got to go," Gage said aloud. *I'll try to feel the agents out before they make it down here and let you know if any of them look fishy.*

That would be all of them, in Nik's opinion, the slimy bastards, but he wasn't about to say that out loud. *Take guards with you,* Nik warned. *And take Janet with you. She has enough magic in her to be able to spin a truth spell and tell if any of these assholes are corrupt.*

Gage smiled. "Yes, Your Highness." He clasped Nik's shoulder before grabbing his mate, who'd been waiting outside the dungeon, the color leeched from her, before heading upstairs.

Nik heaved a heavy, exasperated sigh and ran his hands through his hair. It felt weird to be able to do that now. Sometimes the stuff hung in his eyes and got on his damn nerves, but Alara sure seemed to dig the hell out of it. It was his hair's saving grace. Otherwise, it would have been gone a long time ago.

Alara was silent, looking around in that sharply observant way of hers. She sniffed once, her nose crinkling in disgust.

"What is it?" Nik asked in a low voice.

"The magical residue hanging in the air... it smells... wrong."

He'd noticed it too, a sour, tangy smell that left his sinuses and throat feeling raw. "Must be from the backlash on the spell," Nik murmured, trying to keep his voice down. There were still too many eyes and ears in the room, thanks to the swarm of royal guards and approaching DPI, and Nik didn't know whom they could trust.

"It reminds me a bit of the doppelgänger's scent," Alara said absently, as if she was thinking about one thing while trying to speak about something else.

Come to think of it, it did. Why hadn't he picked up on that? Dammit, he was too distracted by everything.

Get your shit together.

The nagging sense that he was starting to unravel pulsed at the back of his mind, but he wouldn't let himself fall apart. He couldn't. No Alpha could, no matter how much pressure they were under.

The procession of agents stopped in the foyer. Nik

heard Gage tell them Janet, one of Nik's resident wolves who had an affinity for Green Magic, would be scanning them.

One man scoffed, outraged at the implication.

"It's just a precaution," Gage assured them, but with enough steel to let them know this was nonnegotiable.

They began to argue, what Nik presumed to be the head agent going on about how "disrespectful" and "ridiculous" this was.

"Do you think we should hand the doppelgänger over to them?" Alara asked quietly.

Nik pressed his lips together, his eyes narrowing. "She's been nothing but trouble since we got her. Even if… what Gage says about the DPI is true, I think we're better off without her. Let her become their problem."

Alara's shoulders sank slightly, and she turned away. Nik's heart broke a little at her attempt to hide her disappointment.

He hated times like these, when he had to make a decision between being a supportive mate and being a protective Alpha. He always swore his mate would come before his pack, but it wasn't so black and white as that. It couldn't be. He felt each and every imperfect soul of his packmates—their hopes, dreams, desires. Though he didn't know what it felt like yet, he imagined it resembled a parent's love for his children. He'd rip out his heart before causing any of them harm.

"Miss, you must stay down!"

Alara and Nik looked over as the frenetic Blue Warlock hovered and fussed over Penelope. She was starting to come around again, groaning as she wobbled to her feet. "Please, Doctor, I've had worse," she said through gritted teeth.

At the doctor's insistent, exasperated pleas, she shushed and assured him she was fine, only weakened. "Magic drains you," she said tiredly. "This spell much more than usual, I'm afraid," she added with a weak smile.

The doctor threw up his hands as she started toward the door. "I have to report this… to the Council of Magic," she said in a paper-thin voice between raspy breaths.

Nik cut her off. Alara joined him in blocking off the exit. "Hold up there, Pen. You're in no condition to be going anywhere. No offense, but you look like shit."

"None taken. I've come to expect comments like that from you." As if on an afterthought, she turned. Her eyes searched for the girl, at last finding her where she was still slumped in the chair. While the doctor had checked on her to make sure her vitals were stable, no one else had dared touch her yet out of fear of what would happen.

"Has she awoken yet?" Penelope asked. It was a flat question, without warmth or concern. A flicker of hatred rolled through her eyes, which were usually so full of light and love.

Nik's spine stiffened. "Not that we know of, no."

Penelope stared without blinking, her gaze growing distant. "She just collapsed," she said at last. The words were barely audible and pronounced slowly, as if she were reliving what happened. She lifted her hands, turning them over this way and that as she examined them. What she was looking for, Nik had no idea. "I felt a pull before the magic severed and the spell broke. I think… I think someone didn't want us to find out what she knows. Through any means necessary, which probably resulted in her current state. Something went wrong."

"You mean, like someone tried to kill her? To save their own ass?"

Penelope nodded. "Just like when a soldier cracks open a cyanide pill lodged in a fake tooth when the good guys capture him for interrogation."

Which meant their only lead to Mistress Black's whereabouts just went out the door. Damn. This day just kept getting worse and worse.

A shiver rolled over Penelope, and she hugged herself, abruptly tearing her gaze from the doppelgänger. "The DPI are here, I take it?"

"Yeah," Nik said sourly, crossing his arms.

Penelope nodded. "Good. They can take over from here. Though, to be fair, I'm not sure she'll wake up from this."

"You mean she could be in a coma?" Alara asked.

"I don't know." Penelope sighed. "This has never happened to me before, and I'm not sure what caused the spell to backfire. Only time will tell if she'll wake up. Perhaps the DPI has better resources, and they'll be able to revive her." She gave Nik an apologetic smile. "I'm sorry, Nik, Alara. I've botched this up."

"Hey, we're just glad you're all right," Nik said, smiling. "Don't sweat it. I'm not losing any sleep over you knocking that thing out."

Alara grumbled something he couldn't quite make

out, which he was pretty sure was a disagreement accented by some cuss words. He really had started to rub off on her.

"I should try to get back to report what happened to the Council. They'll want to know about this, and I'd rather them hear it from me first before word gets to them," Penelope said darkly.

Nik couldn't blame her there. Every faction of the Underworld had its own set of problems, but the witching community especially could be downright cutthroat. You never knew who was out to get you.

Story of my life.

Closing her eyes, Penelope began to chant softly. A light, silvery glow surrounded her form, twinkling with little diamond lights. It started to grow brighter and then abruptly sputtered and winked out. Penelope tried summoning it again but to no avail. She sighed, rubbing her temples. Bags hung under her dull eyes. "It's no use. I can't teleport. I'm too weak."

"You could stay here. Rest up 'til you're ready to move out," Nik said. "We've got plenty of room."

Penelope considered it silently for a beat before smiling and nodding. "Thank you. I accept."

Nik watched her as a guard, followed by the doctor, escorted her out. Her eyes locked on the doppelgänger once more, malice shining there before she looked away as they disappeared through the door.

His body tensed, and his blood ran cold. And for the first time in his life, Nik was actually afraid of Penelope. Which was as absurd as being scared of the Easter Bunny.

"What's wrong?" Alara asked, gazing at him with a raised brow.

"Nothing." At least, he hoped it wasn't anything to be concerned over.

You're just tired, and this situation has made you paranoid.

Those are the things he told himself as he and Alara left, Nik's eyes pinned to the back of Penelope's head the whole time.

Watching, waiting. For what, he did not know.

And something told him he didn't want to find out.

CHAPTER EIGHT

I f the DPI didn't leave soon, Alara was going to
hit something. Maybe someone, probably one of the
agents.

And wouldn't Nik just love that?

Actually, he would. She knew he would. There was
nothing he'd love more than to drive his fist into the face of
that pompous head agent, Agent Chang. He had a proud
jawline, a mouth that never smiled, and cold, sharp eyes
that always beheld them with condescension, and Alara
was about ready to throw peace and decorum and all that
bullshit to the wind and let her claws out on the man.

If it weren't for Nik's running mental commentary—
*Hey, Officer Asshat here forgot to remove the lipstick stain
from his collar. You think his wife will notice?* Or *Captain
Dickface finally blinked. Maybe he is human*—Alara would
have lost her cool a long time ago. Her fuse had run a hell
of a lot shorter since her parents' and sister's deaths—that

she would admit. The stress of the evening, especially that horrible smell in the woods, those eyeless sockets staring at her accusingly, as if blaming her for the victim's death, only chipped away at what little restraint she had left.

Thank God for Nik.

Penelope—poor, sweet, annoyingly sexy and thin Penelope—had even started to grow snappy after an hour of questioning and magical scans from the DPI. Alara didn't know much about magic, but from the hum of energy in the air, the witches the agency had brought in to work on Penelope were top notch. Aside from Penelope, Alara hadn't encountered signatures that strong. Being in close proximity with that much power was both unnerving and awe inspiring.

The DPI's witches and warlocks scanned Penelope several times, using different techniques and incantations, but no one could unlock her memory. It was as if those precious few minutes in the dungeon had been wiped out. Gone. Poof. Rendered nonexistent.

Alara shivered. That had to be scary, feeling like shit and being unable to remember what had happened to you. Wondering if there was something really wrong.

At one point, they made it back downstairs. The dungeon's surveillance videos as well as the magical floating camera Penelope had summoned had cut out shortly after Penelope had begun her spell. So those were a no-go for figuring out what went wrong with the spell. The DPI also tried, unsuccessfully, to cast a reenactment spell that would show them what had happened in the room. Basically, ghostly figures, or "shadow images," of Penelope and the doppelgänger would reenact exactly what had happened. Alara had been looking forward to seeing that. She'd never heard of such a spell and was bummed when they couldn't seem to be able to get it to work either.

The DPI was running into dead end after dead end, and the frustration levels in the room were slowly elevating until everyone was grouchy as all get-out.

But "Agent Stoneface" was relentless. He needed answers, dammit, and he needed them now.

Only when Penelope began to pass out from exhaustion did the Moonstruck Pack's Blue Warlock doctor, Heath, puff up his chest and demand she rest. Alara had to admit watching Heath and Agent Chang go at it was entertaining for a few minutes.

Heath finally growled a curse, saying he was "doing what was best for his patient," and started hauling Penelope out of the room with the help of another wolf. Agent Chang started to pursue, but Nik intercepted. "I'd be careful, if I were you. I once saw him rip the arm off a doctor who opposed him."

Agent Chang turned white as chalk and swallowed hard. Grumbling about how the witch was useless anyway in this state, he let her go.

Alara suppressed a growl. Useless. Like a piece of machinery that wouldn't work. An object. Was that how the DPI viewed civilians? Their employees?

Alara resolved to glare at him the rest of the evening. As a result, he never much looked at her. Which suited her just fine.

By the time they were finally ushered out of the

dungeon, they still hadn't moved the doppelgänger's body. What the hell were they waiting for? Perhaps they were just as scared of it as the werewolves.

And if the "Underworld's finest and bravest" were afraid...

After more arguing, questions, and spell casting that seemed to get them nowhere, Nik and Alara joined Gage, Danica, and "a whole shitload of agents"—Nik's words, not hers—in the woods.

A nervous tick worked its way through Alara's chest and shoulders, making her jittery and jumpy at every little noise. The woods she'd found so peaceful only a few hours before now felt ominous, as if monsters hunched beneath every shadow, waiting for their next meal.

The group now stood by the body Nik and Alara had uncovered earlier, explaining themselves to the DPI for the umpteenth time.

A leaf fell, brushing her shoulder, and she bit back a screech. Nik, giving her a puzzled look, wrapped his arm around her and pulled her tight. She leaned into him, letting the comfort of his warmth seep into her, drive her fears away.

It was well past 2:00 a.m. before Gage and Danica were dismissed. Though they weren't scheduled to leave for a few days, they opted to go ahead and return home in light of what had happened. He wanted to be at headquarters, at the seat of his power, in case anything happened. He needed his war council to form a plan of action to accommodate these new developments.

Around three, the DPI finally let Nik and Alara retire.

Both were silent as they walked back to the manor and into their shared room.

Nik shut the door, leaning against it while frowning at the floor.

Alara, thinking the bed looked awfully comfy, plopped down on it and fell backward across the comforter. One arm was draped across her stomach, the other lay splayed above her head. She let her eyes drift shut, welcoming the silence and darkness. Ah, it felt good not to think about anything.

Footsteps approached, and a moment later, the mattress dipped beside her. "I'm sorry."

"For what?"

Nik lay down alongside her, drumming his fingers along his stomach and staring up at the ceiling. "I know you're bummed about the doppelgänger. We'll find new leads."

"I know." The reply felt wrenched from her mouth. Her throat had tightened up again.

Damn, why did it seem every time she might actually get somewhere with finding Mistress Black, something always happened to derail her progress? It was growing tiresome. She was exhausted by this never-ending chase. She needed—demanded—justice for her family. And she was running out of leads.

They lay there for a few silent minutes before Nik at last sighed and stood.

Alara sat up. "You're not staying?"

"Can't. There's too many things to take care of, like figuring out how the hell that thing got onto our property in the first place." He leaned down and kissed her. "I'll be up soon."

He started to turn. She grabbed hold of his shirt and yanked him to her in a more passionate kiss. When they at last parted, they were both breathless. "Don't be long," she whispered.

Lust swam in his eyes. Not so discreetly, he adjusted himself; his pants had tightened. "Dammit, woman. You'll be the death of me."

She laughed, and a moment later, he was gone. He cast her a wry smile over his shoulder just before closing the door.

With the room to herself, she got undressed, changed into a lacy nightgown, and lay down. Her eyes closed almost as soon as she nestled beneath the covers. Though exhaustion tried dragging her under, sleep wouldn't quite come. A nervous undercurrent hummed in her veins, bringing worry after worry racing through her head. Taking a deep breath, she concentrated on her breathing and draining her mind of all thought.

She'd always had trouble falling asleep, being the worrywart that she was. Usually, she read a book or watched TV before bed to relax and take her mind off things. As tired as she was, she doubted she'd last very long with either. When Nik couldn't fall asleep one night due to her tossing and turning, she'd finally revealed her problem to him. The inability to shut her mind off. That was when he introduced meditation to her. It was a godsend and worked every time.

It didn't take long before she sank into a deep sleep.

She floated along in quiet darkness, happily surrendering to its promise of peace. That deep, bottomless black consumed her, wrapping her up in a blanket free from worry or fear.

Finally… nothing.

It wasn't even a thought, not really, since she was truly asleep. More like her tired mind sighing with relief to be given a reprieve.

Which, naturally, didn't last for long since this was her life.

Dream-Alara lazily opened her eyes, peering at bright sunlight and blue skies dotted by white, fluffy clouds. Castle Crescent rose to her right, standing guard over the colorful flowers and lush greenery around her.

Fresh spring grass prickled her back; she was wearing her favorite sundress. She could tell by the soft cotton material and the flash of baby-blue fabric she caught from the corner of her eye.

The air smelled like roses, lavender, and a heady mix of other flowers. Her mother's garden always was spectacular in the warmer months.

Bare feet approached. Alara wasn't shocked when her sister sat down beside her. Whole, unmarked by death, pretty in her rose-pink dress and golden curls shining in the sun.

They sat like that for a moment, Izzy gazing out over the rows of neat hedges and trellises fortified with verdant vines and Alara staring up at her sister, trying to capture the moment in her mind like a photograph.

"You're not here," Alara said softly at last. "You're not

real."

"Who says I'm not?" Izzy said, turning to look at her. She wasn't smiling, not really. Her mouth wasn't, anyway. There was a sparkle in her blue eyes, the look she always had when she was alive.

It stung, the realization that this was fake and that she'd never look at her sister's hopeful gaze again. That bright future, gone in a snap.

It wasn't fair. Alara's teeth clenched.

"Of course not," Izzy said aloud. It took Alara a breath to realize Izzy had somehow heard her thoughts. "Life's not fair."

"So you can somehow magically enter people's dreams and read thoughts now?" *That you're dead,* she couldn't bring herself to add.

Izzy's light-pink lips tugged into a small, secretive smile. A bell from a clock tower chimed in the distance.

Strange. Alara didn't remember there ever being a clock tower near.

Izzy frowned, gazing in the direction of the tower. "I don't have long. There are rules, after all." That last part had uncharacteristic bitterness. She went about straightening her dress. Not that it needed it.

Alara frowned. Izzy only hesitated when she wanted to avoid discussing something. Like the time Alara had caught her in the woods one night, lip-locked with one of her father's knights. After the initial embarrassment, both girls had stayed up half the night giggling and swapping juicy details of each other's first kisses. Alara remembered a lot of laughter and happiness from those times.

Tears pricked her eyes. God, she was going to break. Izzy being here was too much.

She hadn't dreamed of her until now, not really. Which made her feel both relieved and guilty. She should dream about her sister. God knew she did enough during the day. But her dreams were strangely blank, void of any color except red.

Death.

Vengeance.

The color to match the anger boiling beneath her skin.

Izzy turned to face Alara, taking her hand and looking her straight in the eyes. "I came here to warn you."

Alara sat up, facing her sister. Izzy didn't kid around, not when she had this serious look about her. Her poker face wasn't that good. The girl had never been a good liar. "About what?" she asked.

"There is an evil approaching, a threat that could tear your pack apart."

Alara laughed. The sound was too sharp, not at all how laughter should be. Must have been because she didn't find the situation funny. "You're a little late there. Evil's already found us." Feeling kind of stupid for being so self-aware during a dream but figuring why the hell not, she spilled the story of the doppelgänger stumbling into the celebration earlier.

Izzy shook her head in frustration. "No, you have it all wrong." Her eyes turned pleading, awash with sorrow. She cupped Alara's cheek. Her fingers were cool despite the warm spring air.

Typical Izzy. Always freezing, Alara thought absently.

Izzy leaned forward, never breaking her gaze. "You, sister. It will be all your fault."

Alara's brows drew up in confusion. "What do you mean?"

Izzy leaned even closer, barely a breath-width away.

"I mean that you're evil."

Alara bolted straight up, violently ripping herself from the dream. Stars flashed in her eyes as her head spun from the sudden movement. Groggy didn't begin to cover how she felt.

A tumultuous storm of emotions assaulted her: anger, confusion, delirium, joy, terror...

You're evil.

Alara pressed a hand to her throat. It had gone dry, making it hard to swallow. She must have been breathing hard during the dream, with her mouth gaping open like a fish's.

God, what the hell was that? At first, she'd been happy to see Izzy—stupid, crazy happy. The happiest she'd been since mating Nik.

And now... now she didn't know what to feel.

Revulsion?

Fear?

Alara stared at her scraped-up and scarred hands. They looked so different now from how they used to a month ago. They looked tougher.

More war ridden.

What had Izzy meant? She was hardly evil. Bitter and enraged from time to time, yeah. Alara wouldn't deny that.

But she defined evil as Mistress Black, Gerard, even

her father, much as it pained her to do so. If she was evil, then she and Izzy, dream or not, had very different definitions of the word.

Heaving a long, deep breath and shaking out her bound-up shoulders, Alara climbed out of bed and padded over to the bathroom for a glass of water. It felt good going down, cool and soothing. She felt even calmer after having drunk it.

She stared at herself in the mirror. *Oh my.* She'd never really paid attention to her reflection until now.

Her complexion had paled, looking almost sickly. Her eyes were bloodshot, which would explain the perpetual stinging throughout the day and night. Her dark hair had even lost its luster and curl. Sometime over the course of the month, it had become a frizzy, unmanageable mess. Another problem she didn't want to think about.

Something wet and cool shone against her cheek. Alara reached up, her fingertips dampening with the tear she had shed during her dream.

Remembering Izzy, how close she'd been, made her start to cry all over again.

Izzy, I miss you.

Just then, the doorknob squeaked slightly, and she heard the bedroom door open and close.

A sob blubbered out before she caught it, reining in her sorrow. She shoved the memory of her sister to the back of her mind, where she knew it would linger. It was useless trying not to think of her family at all; she always did anyway, despite her best efforts at keeping those dead faces locked away, where they couldn't hurt her anymore.

Exhausted and figuring it was Nik anyway, Alara shut the bathroom light off and walked back out into the bedroom. "Did you finish everything you needed to—"

She stopped short.

Because it wasn't Nik standing just inside her bedroom door.

It was Penelope.

CHAPTER NINE

"**W**HAT ARE YOU DOING HERE?" ALARA FINALLY SAID. Her body wouldn't completely relax. *It's just Penelope,* she told herself.

It was of little comfort. Her instincts kept her senses sharp, prepping for escape. Which was ridiculous.

Wasn't it?

Penelope remained eerily still, those silver eyes—

Wait, silver?

Alara searched her memories. No, Penelope's eyes weren't silver. They were this beautiful purple color. She was sure of it.

Or were they blue? Crap, were they actually silver? Panic made her second-guess herself.

Penelope stood there with her hands by her sides. "I just wanted to ask you a question," she said.

There was something off about her voice. It was... dead. Monotone.

As the doppelgänger's had been.

Ice shards penetrated Alara's heart and flooded her bloodstream.

When the spell had backfired… had… She gulped. Had the doppelgänger somehow managed to take over Penelope? She didn't want to believe it was possible. Penelope was so strong, one of the strongest witches out there, Nik had said.

But so little research had been done on doppelgängers, because they could be hard to spot. Some were very good at mimicking their hosts' personality quirks and speech patterns, making them indistinguishable from the originals. The thought of your own family being unable to recognize the real you was scary as hell. You could live most of a lifetime trapped in your own body, crying out for help, and no one would ever be able to hear you.

Alara didn't move. Didn't blink, didn't breathe. She stood rooted to the spot, unable to look anywhere but at the White Witch standing between her and her only way out.

She risked a furtive glance to the side. If she was fast, she might be able to make it out the balcony doors and into the night.

If she was fast. Somehow, she knew the witch would be faster. Magic was funny like that.

Alara tried to speak, but her voice cracked. Swallowing to wet her throat, she rasped, "It's awfully late. I'm tired, and I'm sure you need to rest. Can this not wait 'til morning?"

"It's very important, actually." The same robotic voice. Had Penelope blinked at all in this entire time?

Her eyes had changed colors. They looked normal now.

Blue. Her eyes were the palest blue, to match her dress.

Except they were also flecked with silver now. She was quite certain they hadn't been earlier in the dungeon. No—she was positive. The icy fear in her blood made her so.

Alara felt that she was losing control, her calm facade giving way to terror. A tremble had started in her knees, washing over her body within mere seconds and making her feel stupid and weak.

But she could not—would not—feel weak. She would not give in, not to this monster.

She would fight like hell. For Nik, for herself, for her pack.

Steeling herself, she discreetly shifted her weight to the balls of her feet as she spoke, prepping to run. "We can play this game all night, you know," she said.

"What game is that?"

"The one where we pretend you're still Penelope."

Penelope actually blinked then folded her arms. An attempt to look more human.

Goose bumps broke out along Alara's arms.

"I don't know what you're talking about," Penelope said, this time with more warmth to her voice.

Alara chuckled darkly. "Don't toy with me, monster. I'm not as innocent as I look."

That silvery sheen returned to Penelope's eyes, and she smiled. "I'm counting on it."

Her hand shot out.

Alara immediately dove to the side, the silvery wisp of light whooshing by her foot.

The balcony was her only shot at escaping. She had to reach it, at any cost.

Quickly finding her footing, she bolted for the doors, pushing her body to its limits. The doors exploded open as she shoved them, fresh air kissing her face just long enough to provide her with the hope that she may yet escape this. That she might not succumb to this unholy terror.

Her foot found the cool iron railing, and she jumped, preparing to shift during the fall and land on four paws.

An invisible force, sticky and sweet smelling, yanked her back mid-leap. With a strangled cry, she was pulled back into the room, suspended above her bed by delicate, glowing silver threads. Her body would barely move. She grunted, pulling with all her might. It felt as if she'd been caught in a spiderweb.

Soft heels clicked closer as Penelope strode toward her, staring at her with those damnable silver eyes.

Alara's heart rate accelerated. She thrashed more wildly. "Help!" she screamed. *Nik!*

"No one can hear you. I cast a soundproofing spell over the room before I came in here. Oh, and don't bother calling for your mate. The spell mutes your mate-bond as well."

Fury rolled through her. She would have asked, "What do you want?" if it hadn't been kind of obvious. "You can't have me, monster," she spat instead. "I won't let you take me."

Penelope stepped onto the bed, reaching up to cup Alara's face.

Alara snarled, flinching away, but Penelope's warm hand stubbornly followed. "Sssh," Penelope cooed. The doppelgänger was getting better at imitating her. If not for those silver eyes, Alara would have had a hard time telling the difference at this point. "I don't want to hurt you," Penelope said.

"You're lying. You want to take me over."

"I want to borrow you," Penelope corrected.

"Is there a difference?" Alara said bitterly, refusing to look away, refusing to be cowed by this *thing*.

Penelope's hand dropped away. "There's a very large difference. I only need you for a short period of time."

Oh, that makes it so much better. "For what purpose?"

"That I cannot tell you."

"Of course you can't. And what if I refuse?"

"It will be easier if you don't struggle," Penelope cautioned. "I'm going to do this anyway, with or without your permission. I just feel…" She looked away for a moment. "Less guilty knowing it's okay."

"It's okay?" Alara laughed hysterically. "It's never okay to force someone out of their body!"

"I wouldn't be forcing you out," the doppelgänger said defensively. Or rather, Penelope said. "I just said you can have your body back once I've completed my task."

"And what task is that?" When the thing didn't speak, Alara snapped, "Tell me! I have a right to know!"

"I want to stop Mistress Black."

Alara froze, staring. "You're lying."

"Doppelgängers are descended from the ancient Fey. We cannot lie." She grinned. "Though we can twist the truth more easily than our fairy brethren."

"So you could still be technically lying."

"No, I just might not tell the truth in a way you want to hear it."

That monotone voice, speaking in riddles, in that twisting, winding way of hers. Of course doppelgängers were Fey. Why didn't she see it before?

Probably because you've never met a fairy before.

She'd heard stories—terrible, dark tales of teeth and wings and luminous eyes. None ended well.

Her heartbeat, so strong and swift, felt like the only sensation anchoring her to her body. The moment felt so surreal. "Back in the dungeon you said you were running from Mistress Black. Is that true?"

"Yes," the doppelgänger answered instantly.

"Why?"

Alara didn't think she was going to answer. "Mistress Black captured me once she realized what I was and what I could do. She made me her slave."

"How?"

"Through magic. How else?" she said dryly.

"But you got away."

"Yes. Barely. It almost cost me my life. I managed to slip into the body of one of the witches from her inner circle."

"Inner circle?"

"She surrounds herself with twelve powerful paranormals: witches, warlocks, Fey, werewolves, vampires." She shivered. "And a demon."

Alara swallowed hard, her throat turning to ice. "So you took over a witch. Then what?"

"I used her powers to break the tracking and binding spells on me. Mistress Black had cast them so I wouldn't be able to escape her lair, and if I did, she could always find me."

"But not anymore."

"Not yet."

"What do you mean not yet?"

She sighed. "She's hunting me. I've been outrunning her spies, jumping from body to body. But she's catching up. The only way for me to be free of her is to get rid of her."

"How?" Alara leaned forward against her bonds. "How do you kill her?"

The doppelgänger regarded her silently, and Alara knew she would get no more.

Unless she…

For an irrational moment, she started to consider letting the doppelgänger take control of her body. Her anger and despair begged her to. That witch needed to pay. Hadn't Alara said she'd pay any price to get her revenge?

Then there was the idea of letting someone else take control for a while. Not having to think, not having to feel… it sounded like Heaven compared to the hell she'd endured this past month.

There was one problem—Nik.

The thought of leaving him behind, of not registering the gentleness of his touch or the fire of his kiss. It made her want to cry.

"No."

The doppelgänger blinked. "I'm sorry?"

"No," Alara said more forcefully, staring the doppelgänger down. "You can't use me. It's not okay to take someone else's body."

The doppelgänger smiled softly. There was a hint of admiration in her silvery eyes. "And as I said, you won't have a choice."

Alara opened her mouth to speak again, but she never got a chance to.

Penelope raised her arms and opened her mouth wide. Black, shimmering lines shot out of her fingertips, mouth, and eyes.

Alara had a fraction of a second to realize what was happening before the magic choked out all breath and thought. It crammed itself into her eyes, her mouth, her ears—everywhere. She gagged on it, thrashing around as she literally drowned on Black Magic.

Her lungs began to scream for air.

Oh God. Was she dying?

No. No, not like this. Nik!

Frantic, she tried calling out for her mate once more through their mate-bond. Her cries were met with silence.

Nik's handsome face—the mischievous sparkle to his eyes and wicked tilt of his grin—was the last thing she thought of before blacking out.

She was alone. Unlike before in her dream, the darkness

here was cold and foreign. There was no Izzy to warm her with thoughts of sunshine and better days, no hope of going back to the life she once had at the manor with Nik.

A life, in retrospect, which was wonderful, even if her family was dead.

Wake up, a cool, slithering voice whispered. It echoed in the void, seemingly all around her.

Groaning, she came to. The world blurred and then came into focus. She was lying on the bed. Well, mostly on it. One leg and arm dangled off the side, and her temple throbbed. She reached up to touch her forehead, wincing. The skin was tender. Sitting up, she looked at herself in the gilded mirror hanging over their bed. A new bruise had formed above her left eye. She must have hit her head on the headboard when—

She drew a blank. What had just happened?

She paused. No, she couldn't remember what she'd been doing.

How did she get in here? She remembered preparing for a party to honor the High King and Queen, going to the woods with Nik… and then nothing.

Growling in frustration, she concluded that her brain must be too groggy from exhaustion to be of much use. Stumbling out of bed on shaky legs, she started toward the bathroom when she tripped over something and nearly hit the ground. Catching herself on the footboard, she whirled around.

Alara drew completely still. "Penelope?"

The White Witch lay sprawled on the hardwood floor, limbs in disarray as if she had collapsed.

A flash of something—a memory?—went through Alara's mind.

Penelope standing in the doorway.

Alara making a mad dash out to the balcony, only to be snatched back inside by magic.

Alara silently screaming as Black Magic poured itself into her.

It all came back in a rush. "No," Alara breathed, sinking to her knees and staring at Penelope.

Yes, came the slithering voice inside her head.

Alara shook her head, tears spilling over her eyelids. "No, no, no, no…" She bit back a sob, calming herself with deep breaths, and closed her eyes. Her fists clenched as anger swelled within her, and she commanded, "Get out of my head."

I can't, the doppelgänger said. Alara couldn't tell if it was male or female. Its voice had both high and low pitches to it, as though it were many voices speaking at once. *Once I've left a host, I cannot reenter it ever again.*

Alara felt something poking and prodding in her brain. Memories, things that were a bit hazy because she hadn't thought of them in years, resurfaced out of the blue.

She gasped.

That thing was digging through her most private thoughts and memories.

Faster and faster the doppelgänger sifted, as if cataloging her life, mannerisms, demeanor.

Learning to be her.

Revolted, Alara shouted internally, *Stop!*

The doppelgänger ignored her, continuing its invasion

of Alara's most intimate moments. Pictures of her family cascaded by—thoughts of lonely, cold birthday parties, warmer Christmases filled with her sister's laughter, and dark thunderstorms spent trembling beneath her covers.

The thought of that vile creature laying its claws, fingers, or whatever the hell it had on her memories of Izzy was too much. *Stay the hell away from my family, you bitch!* Alara screamed. Reaching deep inside herself, she wrenched the memories free of the creature, locking them all away in a tight, impenetrable box.

At least, she hoped so. She didn't know what this thing was capable of. Maybe there was no safe haven for her memories, not in her mind, anyway.

She felt the doppelgänger still, studying her. *You're stronger than I thought. No matter. Others have started out strong before, as well, but everyone gives up after a while.*

I won't. I will fight you every single damn day until I find a way to get rid of you for good.

Eerie, multitoned laughter danced about her head. *Others have tried. They failed.*

Again, I won't.

The laughter died away. The doppelgänger inhaled deeply, and Alara shrank back.

How pathetic and strange. She was shrinking away from herself. How did you escape something like this? Something that had burrowed its way into your pores, the very essence of your being?

I can smell your anger, the doppelgänger said. *Can feel its flames licking my skin. It burns as hot as I hoped it would. Excellent. I'm going to need that anger.* It said this with the clinical detachment of someone evaluating a racehorse.

Alara almost couldn't bring herself to ask, she was so nauseous with fright. *What do you want from me?*

Your cooperation, for starters. You help me, I help you. I will release you once this is done.

Once what is done?

Once we've stopped Mistress Black.

Alara wanted to believe it. But could she trust it? She was leaning toward "hell no." This was a creature that had had centuries to practice the art of deceptive truths. A game Alara was no beginner at, thanks to her time at Court.

I can sense your doubt, the doppelgänger said. It sighed. *I can't blame you for not trusting me. But think for a moment, Alara. Don't you want to release all that anger? Don't you want to feel happy again?*

A desperate *yes* almost popped out immediately, but she kept her mental mouth shut.

You should get rid of your anger, and soon. Because if you don't, then believe me—it will devour you. Twist you into something dark and cruel.

Alara thought of early mornings spent with punching bags, imagining they were the faces of her enemies, of nearly choking out the doppelgänger's last host in the dungeon if it didn't tell her what it knew about how to find Mistress Black…

God, who was she becoming? This angry, vengeful person who knew no limits? It felt empowering and frightening at the same time.

Who did she want to be?

She remembered a woman, smiling and cuddling with her mate. A woman who loved him more than life itself and would do anything to be the mate—the queen—he deserved.

Happy, simple things. That was what she wanted.

So why couldn't she just let her anger go? Did she really have to purge it, as the doppelgänger said?

Was there really no other choice?

Nik will be able to sense you're here, Alara said absently. *Inside me.* She gulped, nearly throwing up as she acknowledged it.

My presence will be hidden from your mate. The mate-bond won't be able to sense it.

What about her? Alara gestured to Penelope, who still lay unconscious on the floor.

Ah, the White Witch. She is powerful. And very useful. I almost used her body instead for my purpose.

So why didn't you?

Because you want Mistress Black dead more than she does. For you, it's personal. You'll be more motivated to do as I ask.

Alara couldn't argue with that logic, creepy as it might have been hearing someone talking to her inside her head. Knowing there was something inside of her.

She shivered, hugging herself. *What happens to Penelope?*

I can return her soul to her, though I'm reluctant to let it go. So useful. So powerful. It spoke with the fondness of one admiring a favorite pet. *But I'll only return her soul if you stop fighting me and just do as I ask.*

What happens if you don't return her soul?

She dies, the doppelgänger said simply, almost bored.

Alara's heart skipped. She barely knew Penelope, maybe was even a little bit jealous of her. She was thin and powerful, both things Alara was not. She never seemed to gain a pound, while Alara struggled to keep the weight off. The smoky looks Penelope had thrown Nik hadn't gone unnoticed, either.

No. No, she couldn't let someone die over petty insecurities.

More so, the doppelgänger went on in a darker voice, *if you don't comply, I will ensure your entire pack, your mate—everyone you know and love—dies by your hand.*

Alara stopped breathing. Izzy's words, warning her she would destroy everything dear to her, flashed through her mind.

Was this what she was warning her about? To accept the doppelgänger's presence or risk tearing her loved ones apart?

How do I know you're not lying about Penelope? Alara asked, trying not to let her voice warble. *Don't doppelgängers kill their hosts by pushing out their souls?*

Somehow, Alara knew the creature was rolling its eyes, even though she couldn't see them. It was as if a shadow cloaked it. Or a veil. A long, sinewy veil, dark as midnight. *The mythology surrounding my kind is laughable at times. Doppelgängers can never truly kill their hosts by just inhabiting them. We can't push their souls out, though we can cage them in the host's body. Getting rid of a soul entirely would be impossible for a doppelgänger. But not for something else.*

Alara wondered if it meant a demon, perhaps.

She weighed her choices, the answer becoming unbearably clear. Staring at Penelope and feeling as if she suddenly weighed a ton, she said aloud in a deadened voice, "You can take my body." Her eyes narrowed. "But I will never stop trying to fight you."

You can try, the doppelgänger replied, unfazed. *You're strong, I'll grant you that. But sooner or later, that strength will run out. Many find it easier—preferable, even—to just let me run their lives. It's easier than the toil of living.*

An icy wave of fear rolled through Alara. She'd been thinking the exact same thing earlier, how nice it would be to just let someone else take over for a while. Let them deal with all the pain and suffering.

Was she strong enough to not ever give in? Would she eventually run out of hope, as other hosts had done?

Believe in yourself.

Izzy's voice was soft but insistent, a spark of hope in the darkness. It fueled the growing fire of resistance inside Alara's heart.

You swear you'll leave my loved ones unharmed, you'll return Penelope to her original state, and you'll release me once we've stopped Mistress Black?

Of course. Almost as soon as the words were uttered, Alara's hands rose of their own accord. She gaped at them, feeling like a puppet being led about by strings.

Let's wake our little witch up, shall we? the doppelgänger said sweetly.

Alara felt a rush of power gather at her fingers. Black

Magic crackled around her hands in purple and black sparks. She stared in horror as the magic swelled, darkening and thickening until it was a writhing, globby mess.

Don't, she said, trying to stop it, but it was no use. Terrified, she scrambled to regain control of her body, staring in horror at the terrible magic growing in her hands. *Stop!*

You made your choice. Live with it, the doppelgänger said.

The magic exploded from her hands, driving itself into Penelope. Her spine arched, and her eyes snapped open, her pupils tiny dots within a glowing sea of white. Her mouth had opened in a silent scream as the magic surged along her body.

Through the magic, Alara felt the cage around Penelope's soul begin to quake.

The doppelgänger was keeping its word. It was breaking the cage, releasing Penelope.

Sweat broke out along Alara's brow, and a wave of ice washed through her. Her vision began to turn black—she was going to pass out.

I… can't…

Just a little bit more, the doppelgänger insisted.

Alara heard a snap, felt Penelope's soul break free. The witch's body fell to the ground, lying still, the subtle rise and fall of her stomach the only sign she was alive.

The magic abruptly sucked back up into Alara, and her body began to spasm, short-circuited by the magic it wasn't used to invoking.

The sensation of floating came over her, and Alara

smiled as she collapsed.

Her eyes fluttered closed, and a slight smile pulled at her lips.

Ah, there it was.

Rest. Someone else was in charge. Yeah, let someone else deal with all this for now. The anger, the pain, the grief, the pack… Alara was so very, very tired.

It will be all right soon, a dark voice promised, and then Alara thought of nothing.

CHAPTER TEN

L EAVING HIS MATE BEHIND WAS NEVER EASY FOR NIK. When she smelled like sex, it was damn near impossible.

Growling internally at his responsibilities for getting in his damn way again, Nik had done his best to ignore his raging boner and forced himself to walk away.

Duty calls.

Nik should have been used to it by now. His pack and his mate were supposed to be equal because they were all part of his "family." But since becoming Alpha, he'd found more and more that the pack demanded greater attention. It was the equivalent of dealing with a brood of needy kids over spending time with his mate.

Which was all part of the reason why Nik never wanted this job in the first place. *Dammit, Gage.* Always sacrificing for his baby brother's welfare.

Despite his disgruntlement, he knew he'd keep doing it over and over again. It was what he'd been doing since they were kids. Nik defending Gage from bullies at the school playground, Nik taking the beating from their dad for Gage accidentally breaking a dish, or Nik clawing and biting his way through the bloody and violent nights under Malachite's rule.

He knew Gage had felt guilty. Still did. And, in typical Nik fashion, he would console his brother and put on a good show of not giving a damn to make all of Gage's worries go away.

Because that was what big brothers did.

Just as Alphas looked after their pack, their "little brothers and sisters."

Starting with finding out what the hell the perimeter guards had been doing when that freaking doppelgänger slipped onto their property.

Nik didn't need to look at his guard duty chart to know who had been working the inner, middle, and outer lines. He'd picked the men himself, going only with those who had some experience with the woods. Hunters, trackers—hell, even a hiker—anyone intimate with the inner workings of a forest.

He suppressed a yawn as he stepped into the night once more, wishing he'd gone for a Red Bull before setting out for this. Despite it being nearly dawn, he knew he'd never be able to sleep well without getting all of his affairs in order. It was a trait he and Gage shared—a nervous tic, if you will. Sometimes, like tonight, it came in handy, but most of the time it was just a pain in the ass.

His eyelids started to droop as sleep whispered seductively to him, but he told it to fuck off. He had shit to do.

"Ah, there you are."

Nik didn't even bother suppressing his groan. He was past the point of giving a damn.

Son of a bitch, he'd really been hoping to avoid these guys. Especially this one.

Agent Asshole approached, his fancy suit still looking spotless despite his trekking around in the woods. Probably "supervising" instead of doing any real work, lazy dickwad.

Dickwad? What are you, five? Even his insults were getting lamer the more tired he got.

"Listen," Nik said straight away, "whatever you're about to ask me, it'll have to wait. I don't have time for this right now."

Agent Chang whistled low. "And I thought only vampires were touchy this close to dawn."

So not in the mood. "The hell you want?"

Agent Chang chuckled. For a second, his eyes flashed silver.

Nik blinked. *Must be the moonlight.* And his sleep-deprived brain making up shit that wasn't there.

"I just wanted to go over a few details, if you don't mind."

As if I have a choice, Nik thought dryly.

Agent Chang took out his notepad, cuing an eye-roll from Nik. The tip of a fancy pen popped out, along with a tight smile directed once again toward the wolf. "Less than two months back, you were involved with a shoot-out at a warehouse. And an attack at a motel over in Tennessee, one at Castle Crescent, and now this doppelgänger business."

"And?"

"Well, all these events are linked somehow to Mistress Black. You seem to be at the middle of this war."

"Just what are you suggesting?"

He smirked. "Just that it's awfully interesting. What would a centuries-old Black Witch want with a bunch of country-bumpkin werewolves?"

Nik let the insult roll off of him. It wasn't the first time someone had tried putting their pack down, and it wouldn't be the last.

Child's play.

"I don't know, Agent Chang," Nik said curtly. "That sounds like your job to figure out, not mine. You must really be grasping for straws if you're asking me for help." He shot him his tight smile right back. "Or maybe you're just incompetent, as I've suspected all along."

Chang's eyes flared with fury. A tiny rip drew Nik's eyes to the notepad. Agent Chang had gripped his pen so hard that he'd pressed it clear through the top few sheets of paper.

"You know, you've had a chip on your shoulder the whole night," he said, standing closer. Those sharp eyes of his bored into Nik's.

"Only when it comes to you," Nik said with a smile.

Agent Chang studied him. "No, it's not just me. You don't like the DPI as a whole. Wonder why that is," he mused aloud, slowly. Suspiciously. "Most criminals don't like us either."

"Am I a criminal now?"

"I don't know. But I'm going to find out, one way or

another."

Damn, he did not have time for this cat-and-mouse bullshit.

If he disappeared into the woods, Agent Prick would follow him. Going back to the manor was his only escape route. He'd seen the anxious glances and shifting-weight thing Agent Chang did while inside the manor. Being inside the wolves' den, so to speak, made him antsy, uncomfortable.

Good.

Questioning his perimeter guardsmen would have to wait. Which was fine. He had other work he could do.

He turned to leave without saying a word.

"Hey!" Chang called out. "Where the hell do you think you're going? I'm in the middle of an interrogation!"

"Is that what this was?" Nik called lazily over his shoulder. "Sounded more to me like you were wasting my time. Come back when you have some real questions that are pertinent to figuring out why a dead body and a doppelgänger were on my land."

As he walked away, he waited, listening for Chang to follow. There was swearing, some papers being roughly shuffled, and then Chang walking away.

Nik's shoulders slackened. Thank God for that. He didn't know how much longer he could tolerate these assholes before he went Big Bad Wolf on someone.

He strode to his study, nodding at the front-door guards and the werewolves who passed him in the hallway. It might be late at night, but wolves didn't care. They ruled the night, in a way those vampire pussies only thought they did.

Nik flipped his Do Not Disturb sign over, flashing its menacing red letters for all to see. Being a bit of a nerd, he'd had it custom made online. It read, "DO NOT DISTURB UNLESS A) SOMETHING IS ON FIRE; B) SOMEONE IS DYING; C) MISTRESS BLACK IS HERE. IN WHICH CASE, COME AND GET ME BECAUSE I WANT TO RIP HER DAMN HEAD OFF."

Usually, he had an open-door policy, where his pack could come and speak with him as needed. He wanted to show them he cared and all that fuzz. But tonight, he needed to be alone. He was about two questions away from exploding on someone, he was that tightly wound. And with his relationship with his pack being strained enough as it was, thanks to the wraith disaster, he didn't want to set anyone off. Some of those wolves were ticking time bombs Nik had yet to figure out how to defuse.

One thing at a time.

Alone at last, he leaned against the door and closed his eyes, soaking up the serenity of the silence. He thought it would soothe him.

If only.

Worry after worry poured through his head, free to roam now that his brain wasn't occupied by Agent Pain in the Ass.

He could feel his muscles drawing tighter, tighter, tightertightertighter—

"Fuck." In a few long strides, he was in front of the wet bar, pouring himself a glass of whiskey. It went down hard and fast, burning the whole way.

Another. He gulped it as if it were water and he were dying of thirst.

Going to pour his third glass, he stopped, breathing heavily. A trio of empty bottles—top-shelf rum, vodka, and te-kill-ya—sat on a corner of the bar, all drunk some-time this week. It hadn't dawned on him just how much liquor he'd had until he'd actually stopped and looked.

Damn it.

Resentfully dumping what he'd already poured back into the bottle and twisting the cap on, he slumped down into his desk chair and ran a weathered hand over his face.

He did not need to get in the habit again of drowning his worries in a bottle. He'd drunk like a fish in his younger years, so drunk on most days he'd end up pissing where he was sleeping. Often wake up in a puddle of his own vomit too.

Alara didn't need that kind of man. She needed his strength right now, not some pussy that looked for an ex-cuse, any excuse, to drink himself into oblivion. Besides, if he started now, he knew he'd binge because it had been so long since he'd allowed himself to get good and ham-mered. To surrender himself to the alcohol, let it take his worries off his shoulders. Recovering from alcoholism wasn't a one-time *BAM! We're done, I'm cured* kind of thing. It was a lifelong commitment.

And clearly, he was struggling.

"Fuck me." He had to find another way to handle stress. Take up croquet or something.

He snorted, imagining himself all spiffed up in a polo and some pressed khakis.

His thoughts drifted again to Alara. Maybe he should just go to bed, take her up on her offer. Now *there* was an extracurricular activity he could wholeheartedly devote himself to. Sex as therapy. He liked the sound of that.

His teeth nibbled his lip as he zoned out, thinking. Well, more like worrying. As usual.

The time he'd spent with his mate in the woods earlier had been fantastic on so many levels. They'd both needed it, needed that closeness, needed to know that even if the world was falling apart, they were still there for one another. But that look in her eyes, the rage and grief and agony there… He wished he could take it all away. If there were any way to keep her from hurting, he would do it, no questions asked and no second thoughts.

But he knew no matter how much he wanted to help, there were some wounds that only you could fix. Alara was strong. He'd seen her strength grow from when she'd arrived as a shunned princess to becoming a queen in her own right. She was a hell of a lot stronger than people, him included, gave her credit for. She could overcome this.

And if she ever stumbled, he'd be there to help carry her the rest of the way. The love he felt for her burned bright in his chest.

To hell and back. That was how far he'd go for her.

His cell phone rang, starling him. "The fuck…?" he muttered. Who the hell was calling at this hour? Digging his phone out of his back pocket, he checked the screen.

Gage.

With a small grin, he put the phone to his ear. "What are you doing up? Don't High Kings have bedtimes?" The joke sounded worn out. So did Gage's reply.

"Speak for yourself, Your Highness."

"Yeah, yeah. I guess I've earned that, with all these months I've given you shit over your title. You Royal Prick."

"Cultured Asshat."

Nik snorted. Cultured. Now there was a word Nik had never heard associated with him. "Good to hear from you, little bro." It felt comfortable saying that nickname, like wrapping yourself up in your favorite old blanket. Warm and familiar. He'd stopped calling Gage "little bro" when Gage had kicked Malachite's ass and had claimed the title of Alpha. He figured if anything officially made him a man, that bit of awesome sure as hell did.

"Likewise," Gage said softly, as if remembering all the times they'd had together. "Have the DPI found anything else?"

Nik smiled softly. *To the point.* He gave his brother a brief summary about the runaround he'd gotten as well as an update on Penelope. "I made her stay here tonight. She was so tapped, she couldn't summon enough magic to teleport or whatever the fuck it is they do out of here."

"Damn." Gage's voice was laced with worry. "I've never seen Penelope struggle to perform magic."

"Me, either, bro. Whatever happened must have been bad."

"They still don't know what caused the reaction in the spell?"

"Penelope couldn't remember what went on. It's like her mind went blank."

Something tugged at Nik's brain, tickling it. Almost as if someone was calling out his name…

Briefly worried, he checked his mate-bond. The line was silent. Alara must be asleep.

Fuck. He ran a hand over his face. This exhaustion shit was starting to get to him. He needed a vacation, but he knew that was wishful thinking.

Gage and he talked more about Penelope before moving on to other topics. Gage hadn't been able to find out much of anything on his end to help his brother, which Nik could tell clearly frustrated him. His heart swelled. Gage could be a teddy bear as well as a badass wolf, always looking out for the interests of others before his own. It was part of what made him such good Alpha, and High King, material.

Nik inquired about Danica. "She's fine," Gage said, with the smile to his voice he always got when talking about his mate. "She passed out in the car on the way back, and she immediately went to bed when we arrived."

"Immediately?" Nik said dryly.

He could imagine Gage's grin. "Well, you know. Almost."

Nik snorted. "Horndog."

"Speak for yourself."

"Sire!"

The door to his study burst open, and a haggard man stood there. He was one of the guards posted outside Alara's room.

Nik immediately shot to his feet. "What is it?"

"Lady Alara," the breathless wolf heaved. "She's been

found unconscious in your room. We thought we heard something and tried to get in. When she didn't respond, we kicked the door in."

Nik barely gave the man time to finish. He leapt from the desk at once and tore out of the room as if his hair were on fire. "Got to go. Alara," he barely said before snapping the phone shut and shoving it in his pants pocket.

He flew through the manor, winding around hallways and nearly slamming into walls as he made a mad dash for the stairs that would take him to his mate.

Alara, Alara, he kept thinking, over and over. The thought of her lying there, her throat slashed or worse, kept replaying in his mind in grotesque, vivid color.

He pushed himself faster, taking the steps two at a time until he came to their bedroom door. It was open. Heath was kneeling beside Alara, who lay as still as snow on the floor.

Nik froze at the sight of her, his heart stopping briefly, before he crossed the room. "What happened?" he bellowed, falling on his knees beside his mate and cupping her cheek. She looked pale, and her skin felt cool and clammy.

Heath looked exhausted from tending to Penelope earlier. His weary eyes regarded Nik solemnly. "She has symptoms of magic exhaustion."

"What? How? She doesn't have any magic."

"So far as we know. But I ran a scanning spell, and it picked up"—he gulped—"traces of Black Magic."

Nik's heart bottomed out. All thought stopped, as though someone had thrown a wrench in the cogs of his brain, rendering it useless for a few seconds. He shook his head, trying to make sense of what the doctor had just told him. "Are you sure?"

"Yes. Positive." His face grew haunted. "There is no mistaking that dark power."

Nik stared at Alara, his beautiful, sweet, good mate. "Could there be some other explanation for her having Black Magic residue or whatever it is?"

"Possibly. Any number of theories could explain it—contamination from another source, infestation—"

"Infestation?"

"Some magic can go rogue, taking on a mind of its own. It can literally infest the cells of another being, much like a bacteria or virus would. Black Magic is especially volatile, second only to Fire Magic."

"So... she could just be sick with magic?" Boy, did his head hurt now.

"It's rare, but it does happen."

"How?"

"Any number of ways, much the same way humans become ill. She comes into contact with something contaminated with Black Magic, it gets in a cut, or she rubs her eyes after touching something with Black Magic."

Nik remembered Alara choking out the doppelgänger. Could that thing have Black Magic? "Did you sense anything on the doppelgänger earlier?"

"No. My scanner didn't pick up anything."

Nik frowned. His spine went rigid.

Oh, holy fuck. Was that body in the woods contaminated with Black Magic? Had he somehow gotten some on him when he'd pulled it free of the tree roots, only to contaminate his mate later?

His blood ran cold, and the snack food he'd had at the celebration earlier turned sour in his stomach.

A soft groan caught his ear. His attention snapped onto his mate, who was slowly coming to.

He let out a long breath, cradling her face in his hands. "Hey, baby. Can you hear me?"

She blinked several times as those beautiful, long-lashed eyes fluttered open and at last focused on him. "Nik?" she rasped, her voice scratchy as hell. "What happened?"

"That's what we're trying to figure out. The guards thought they heard something. When you wouldn't answer the door or respond, they broke in and found you unconscious on the floor."

"They what?" She looked around, surprise on her features. With a hiss, she gritted her teeth and clutched at her temples. "God, my head's pounding."

"Looks like you hit it on something," Nik said softly, gently touching a bruise the size of a baseball above her left eye. "The bed post maybe, when you went down?"

"I… I don't remember."

Nik and Heath glanced at one another. Both were wearing their "what the hell?" looks.

At last, Heath sighed. "I can help with that, I think. Let me try a revival spell, see if we can jog those memories loose."

She eased away from him, eyeing his raised hand warily.

"It won't hurt, I promise," he assured her.

Nik placed a hand on the small of her back for support, letting her know he trusted the doctor. He'd been there since Malachite's days, patching, repairing, and in general performing medical fucking miracles. Many wolves most likely wouldn't have lived to howl at another moon had he not been so damned resilient and good at his job.

Alara's spine relaxed into Nik's palm, and he nodded at the doctor.

Taking a deep breath and slowly letting it out through his mouth, Heath raised his hands slightly and began the incantation in whisper-soft tones. Shimmering royal-blue lights floated out of his fingers, the Blue Magic looking like streams of crystalline water flowing smoothly toward Alara. She tensed as the strands curved upward, pouring into her head.

Her eyes took on a blue hue, shimmering as the spell flowed through her brain, looking for the memories she couldn't recall.

The blue in her eyes flickered with silver, harsh and cold, and the muscles in her neck went taut. Her eyes narrowed, flashing gold as the wolf growled in warning, "Stay out of my head."

Nik watched her carefully. "Alara…?"

A snarl erupted from her throat, and she swiped with her hand. "I said get out!"

The magic dissolved into nothing as the doctor fell back with a cry, clutching at his cheek. Blood dribbled between his fingers in oozing streams from the four lacerations Alara's claws had dug in his face.

Nik's jaw dropped. He stared at Heath, speechless, as did the two guards standing close to the doorway.

His head swiveled, and his eyes landed on his mate, whose chest was heaving as she glowered at the doctor.

He waited for her to come to her senses, for horror to wash over her face as she realized what she'd done, but it never came. Her eyes, so dark and foreign to him, stared with loathing at the man who'd tried to help her.

"Um, I think I'm going to refer you to a specialist in Celera," Heath stuttered, rising quickly to his feet. Celera, population of about three hundred thousand, was about half an hour's drive from Moonstruck. The doctor's hands flew all over his torso, as if to make sure she hadn't laid him open anywhere else. "I'll schedule an appointment for tomorrow, midday, if that's all right?"

"First thing available is fine," Nik said absently, his brain working in Alpha mode while the mate side of him recovered from shock. "The morning is preferable. The sooner the better."

"Of course, of course," Heath muttered, backing away. He never turned his back to them as he quickly left the room, leaving all his supplies by their bedside.

"Leave us," Nik clipped.

The guards didn't question him. After the door clicked shut and Nik sensed they were alone, he sat in silence for a beat with his mate.

"Alara," he finally said. "Talk to me."

She blinked hard then peered up at him in confusion. Her eyes had cleared. "Where is everyone?" Her dark hair swished around her head as she looked about.

"You mean you don't remember?"

"Remember what? What's going on, Nik?"

What the hell? Using as much sensitivity as he could, he explained them finding her and the doctor's failed attempt at jogging her memory. Alara's eyes widened when he told her what she'd done, and her hands flew to her mouth.

"Oh my God," she breathed, shaking her head in denial. "I couldn't—I didn't know what I was doing. Oh God, Nik, I have to find him. I have to apologize." She gripped the bed and started to rise, but her knees gave out. She sank to the floor with a cry, banging her elbows in the process when she fell forward.

"You're not going anywhere," Nik said, grasping her and helping her to her feet. He guided her toward the bed. She felt so light, so weak.

While he tucked her in, his mind barreled toward freak-out mode. *What's happening? What's wrong with her? Was it something I did? Why is she so weak?*

Alara shivered, squeezing her eyes closed. That was right. She'd said she had a headache.

Retrieving some aspirin and a tumbler of water from the bathroom, he helped Alara get the pills down before lying down beside her.

She turned to him, nuzzling her head against his shoulder. He pulled her closer, draping one arm around her protectively. One hand stroked her hair while the other held her as she trembled. It only made him draw her in closer.

"What's wrong, love?" he whispered.

He could smell the salt of tears, which had begun to pour freely down her cheeks, soaking into his shirt. "I don't know what's come over me. Since… since they died, I don't recognize the person I've become." A sob tore at his heart. "I don't want to be this person anymore."

"Sssh." He kissed her forehead, being careful not to press the bruise. "It's all right. We'll get through it together. I swear."

She hiccupped, not saying anything more. Even after she'd cried herself to sleep, he didn't let her go, couldn't leave her there.

Fuck his responsibilities. Fuck the DPI. And fuck that doppelgänger bitch.

He was staying right there and not leaving his mate's side until they found out what the hell was wrong with her memory.

Sometime around dawn, after another hour or so of lying awake, brooding over everything, he at last passed out from exhaustion.

No sooner did his soft snoring fill the room than Alara's eyes slowly opened, alert and ready.

The doppelgänger curled Alara's mouth into a smile, the promise of death making her dark eyes glimmer in the early-morning light.

CHAPTER ELEVEN

ALARA SLEPT AFTER NIK CLIMBED INTO BED WITH HER, or at least she thought she did. She remembered the first kiss of sunlight bathing the windows before another wave of exhaustion hit and took her under. She rode the current, flowing smoothly through the darkness until she lay on soft grass. Spring filled the air, the smell of a hundred wildflowers, soil, and—pollen.

Her dream self woke up with a sneeze.

Izzy gave her a sheepish look from beside her. They were in their mother's garden again. "Sorry," Izzy said. "I guess I made it a bit too realistic." She waved her hand in a graceful sweep, and Alara's nose instantly stopped itching.

"I didn't know you could have allergies in a dream," Alara said dryly, propping herself up on her elbows. She looked around, wishing she had something to wipe her nose off on.

Izzy produced a handkerchief.

Alara wasn't even going to ask. "Thanks," she murmured, taking it and dabbing at her nose.

"So you made this world?" Alara asked, unsure whether or not to offer back the handkerchief.

Izzy waved her away. "Keep it. And sort of, in a manner of speaking. I created it in your mind based off your memories of the place. I can only take you to somewhere you've been before."

Weird. The whole situation was bizarre. Doppelgängers, amnesia, talking to her dead sister in her dreams…

"So are you here to tell me how evil I am and that I'm going to destroy my pack?" Alara asked, sitting up all the way.

"No." Izzy turned to face her head on, a serious look about her delicate face. "I'm here to tell you not to give in."

"Give in to what? Izzy, what are you talking about?"

Izzy shook her head in frustration. It didn't suit her, not her little sister who was full of smiles and goodwill. "Its presence is messing with your mind, affecting your memory. If you don't resist, you may lose yourself forever."

"Lose myself? To what? You're not making any sense."

"The doppelgänger," Izzy said sharply. "Do you remember anything at all? Think, Alara."

Alara scrunched her face up in concentration but still couldn't remember anything before she'd gone to their bedroom to lie down. Slowly, bits and pieces of darker memories trickled into her brain: her trying to escape, her clawing the doctor, her seeing Penelope standing in her doorway. They didn't make sense, but she couldn't put them in the right order because they were too jumbled and coming in too fast.

She remembered a dark voice whispering seductively inside her head…

Alara stared at her hands, her chest. "The doppel-gänger," she whispered. "It's inside of me."

Izzy clasped her hands, her voice desperate. "You need to fight it if you have any hope of surviving this."

"I don't want to fight." It slipped out before Alara could think, a knee-jerk reaction that was as truthful a reply as she could give. "I don't want to worry anymore. Let someone else be in control. My life feels so chaotic and out of balance. I just want someone else to lead, to take it all away."

"No, you don't," Izzy snapped. "You need to find the strength of will I know is in there and use it to get this thing out of you. Do you hear me? Alara? Alara!"

Alara came to abruptly, startled out of the dream by arguing voices at the door.

A quick survey of the empty bed to her left let her know Nik was already up. He stood at the door, bare chested and in his jeans from last night, growling at someone dressed in a suit whose face she couldn't quite see.

"Fine," Nik snapped. "I'll be right there." He slammed the door in the person's face and stalked across the room to their bathroom. He paused when he saw Alara watching him. "Sorry, love," he said, crossing the room toward her. He rushed to her side as she sat up, helping her. "I didn't mean to wake you."

"It's fine." She gave him a quick kiss on the mouth. "What's going on?"

"It's the DPI. They said they've identified the body in the woods. They want me to come out there, but I don't know why the fuck they couldn't just tell me here."

"You should go," Alara said, though she hadn't meant to. The words came out of her mouth without her having to think them. Or, really, without her having to concentrate on saying them.

Chills crept up her arms, but she remained smiling tiredly at her mate.

Nik kissed her forehead and brushed the wisps of dark hair from her face. "I'll be back soon to check on you."

"Okay." She smiled as she watched him throw a shirt on, splash some water on his face, and then leave.

Get up. Now, the doppelgänger said in her mind.

It startled her at first; she'd almost forgotten it. *There's something about you that's making me forget things,* she thought, speaking to it. *The same thing happened to Penelope.*

Alara got up and walked to the bathroom, her body moving of its own accord as she got ready.

My presence isn't natural, the doppelgänger admitted. *Short-term memory tends to be affected first. The longer I stay inside my host, the more I start to impact their long-term memory.*

Alara kept moving, directed by the doppelgänger as she went to the closet and pulled on a black T-shirt and some jeans. Her insides felt frozen as she thought of the implications. *That's how you can live out a lifetime in a host. They eventually forget who they are.*

More or less, the doppelgänger said carelessly.

Anger surged. *I won't let you do the same to me.*

Relax, young wolf. I have no intention of staying in your body forever. Wolves were never to my tastes. It shuddered. *I just need to borrow you for a bit, then I'll find another host.*

So you keep telling me.

It doesn't matter to me if you believe me or not. It is what it is. Hurry up. We must move quickly. Your dawdling is costing us time.

I'm not dawdling. You're the one controlling me.

But you're resisting. It's harder.

Alara didn't realize she was resisting. Maybe Izzy's warning had sunk into her subconscious mind and was resisting the doppelgänger for her.

Good. A hidden thought, a whispered victory. She had the sense that the doppelgänger couldn't see her dreams or hear all of her thoughts. All the better for her. She refused to surrender completely to this thing. She knew she didn't want to, on some deep, carnal level based off of survival.

Why are you in such a rush? Alara asked as she pulled on some tall boots.

Because there is someone in a town not far from here we need to find. But they won't be there for long. They have something we need.

What are we getting?

You'll see.

Alara gritted her teeth. *I'm getting tired of your cryptic messages.*

That's your problem. Now, write this down and leave it on your pillow.

Alara fought the doppelgänger's control, remaining still. *Not until you tell me what the hell we're going after.*

She could almost sense the doppelgänger smile. *Fine—a warlock. He possesses the dagger used to kill your family. That's what we're going after.*

Alara gasped out loud. *Do you mean we're going to meet Gerard?*

No. He's been disposed of. We'll get the dagger from a different warlock.

Her heart pounded. It was too good to be true. The man who'd killed her baby sister... How many times had she imagined curling her fingers around his throat, squeezing until the life left his eyes?

And yet she didn't feel better. She hadn't been the one to kill him. Someone else had robbed her of her chance, her privilege.

Which was ludicrous. What made her think she had the exclusive right to take another person's life? How vain was she? *How did he die? Who killed him?* she asked.

Another witch. Let's just say he died a very painful, excruciating death. The doppelgänger practically purred in satisfaction, making Alara shiver.

Why do we need the dagger?

I told you—to stop Mistress Black. It tried making Alara walk to the door, but she dug her heels in. *You want your revenge on her? The witch who turned your life upside down?* the doppelgänger said. *I will give it to you, if you'll just trust me.*

I don't trust anyone. Well, except Nik. And Gage and Danica. Most royal werewolves tended to have a small list of true allies. It kind of came with the territory.

A wise mantra to live by, the doppelgänger said. *But ask yourself this: Would you be able to sleep tonight knowing that the opportunity to destroy Mistress Black, to save your loved ones from meeting the same fate as your family, had been so close and you'd let it slip through your paws?*

Alara immediately knew the answer. It came in the form of a sinking sensation at the pit of her stomach.

Grabbing a pen and paper from the elegant writing desk in the corner, Alara scribbled the doppelgänger's message. Not that she had much of a choice. It seemed to be getting pushier as it grappled with her for full control.

That's a good wolf. Now, jump out the window and go to the garage. Stay hidden.

Alara deftly leaped off the balcony after checking to make sure the guards had left to rotate their shifts. Slinking through the bushes, she crept along the side of the manor until she came to the garage. She ducked behind a tree and peered around the trunk. *There's someone there. A guard.*

Don't worry about him. Just go toward the Subaru on the corner there, bottom level.

The parking garage was multilevel and large enough to hold fifty vehicles. Attached to the main house, it was easily half the size of the manor.

The security guard stood at his station at the front, which was a cozy little office that held all the keys. Alara approached it, glancing over her shoulder to make sure no one saw her go inside.

The man, a friendly wolf in his sixties named Wayne, looked up from his security footage. At least someone was doing their job. He smiled at Alara and stood, looking puzzled as the door clicked shut behind her. "Your Majesty," he said, making a fist over his heart and bowing. "I'm honored, but I thought you were incapacitated at the moment?"

The doppelgänger seized complete control of her body before Alara could stop it. "You thought wrong," she said in a low voice, her eyes flashing silver.

Wayne's eyes widened as she shot forward, bringing the edges of both her hands down hard on either side of his neck. There was a stunned choking noise, and then his eyes rolled back in his head as he collapsed. The doppelgänger, still in control of Alara's body, caught him and eased him to the ground.

Shock briefly gave Alara back her control over her body. She gaped at the guard, at her hands, then back again. "What the—how did I just—?"

Irritated, the doppelgänger yanked back its control. *Keep quiet, and trust that I know what I'm doing! I won't let any harm come to your body.*

Alara placed two fingers to Wayne's neck, checking his pulse, and then ducked her ear next to his nose to make sure he was still breathing. Words in a strange language she didn't recognize whispered from her lips. Faint blue sparkles popped over the guard's head before evaporating. Alara jerked her hand back. *What was that? What did you do?*

Relax. It's a simple memory spell—

A memory *spell?*

To make him forget only that he saw you, the

doppelgänger quickly amended before Alara had a complete meltdown. She seized Alara's hand and waved it over the DVR and televisions of the security system. Sparks shot out of the equipment, followed by puffs of smoke. A single white spark bolted up the power line and across the garage. *To kill the other cameras and equipment that might have seen us,* the doppelgänger said.

Hey! Alara said indignantly. *That was state of the art! I expect you to replace it.*

She imagined the doppelgänger rolling its eyes as it forced her to stand up. *I think saving the world is payment enough.*

Alara grumbled her response, which wasn't quite audible.

She scanned the wall of car keys, checking each label until she found the key fob for the blue 2014 Subaru BRZ she was looking for.

Snatching it off the wall, she started toward the door, but Alara cried out, *Wait! Will he be all right?*

Growling, the doppelgänger forced her through the door. She briskly walked toward the Subaru parked at the far front corner of the lowest level of the garage. *He'll be fine. We only knocked him out. He'll have a headache when he wakes up, which, by the way, should be soon. Now move.*

With a push of a button, Alara unlocked the car and got inside. The garage staff loved their jobs, fixing and detailing pretty cars. The sleek black interior gleamed from fresh Armor All, and the smell of pine-scented air fresheners filled the cabin.

Alara pressed the start/stop button, and the engine

purred to life.

Let me drive, the doppelgänger said, taking control as Alara switched into reverse.

Alara hovered below the surface of her consciousness, just in case the doppelgänger decided to pull a *Fast and the Furious* and get them both—or someone else—killed. *You're really impatient,* she said. *You know that?*

To her surprise, the doppelgänger's driving was calm—much calmer than Alara's probably would have been. They drove out of the garage at a considerate pace, easing onto the paved driveway and toward the highway.

The doppelgänger fed the engine more gas once they hit the highway. *No one's ever told me that before,* it grumbled.

Once Alara saw the doppelgänger wasn't going to wreck the car, she relaxed a little.

Only a little.

So where are you taking me?

You'll see.

Alara sighed. *Why am I not surprised?*

CHAPTER TWELVE

SON OF A BITCH, HE WAS LOSING HIS DAMN MIND.

It didn't help that he was cranky when he first woke up anyway. He was downright uncivil when it was the ass crack of dawn and he wasn't buried under his bedsheets.

By nature, Nik was a night owl, as were most of his pack members. He and his board of advisers held most of their business meetings at night, often going as late as 1:00 or 2:00 a.m.

Nik and Agent Asshole had been wandering around the woods for the past fifteen minutes, seemingly going nowhere. More than once, Nik offered—yeah, yeah, through gritted teeth, but hey, at least he was attempting to be polite—to just use his wolf nose to sniff out the body site. And every time, Chang insisted it was "just over here" or "he was just a little turned around."

By a little, you mean miles, dipshit, Nik wanted to say but bit his lip.

Mostly, he just didn't think the pompous ass wanted to lower himself to accepting help from a werewolf, but what the fuck ever. Captain Stick Up His Ass was going to have to get over that shit soon, because Nik was running out of patience.

Nik's temper was nearing explosive levels when they crested a hill and there stood the crew, about half a mile away. "Ah, there they are," said Chang, carefully making his way over to them. "I told you they were around here."

Nik grumbled more expletives, too softly for the agent to hear, as they drew up to the rest of the crime investigation crew.

"Dyson," Agent Chang barked, "give us a report."

A young blond man with freckles and huge round glasses looked up, startled. "Uh, yes, sir!" He waved awkwardly at Nik, smiling a little. "Agent Nick Dyson," he said in a voice that was slightly high pitched. Nik grasped his hand firmly in a quick shake, the kid's nerves seeping into him. "Only, I spell mine with a C between the I and the K."

Nik raised a brow.

"Um, right," Nick with a C said, turning to the corpse. "I'm the guy that examines the victims at the crime scene. What we've found out so far is that she's—well, was—a witch. A generalist, for the most part, with a knack for hypnotism."

"Hypnotism?"

"Yes. A very niche type of magic. She went missing from Savannah, Georgia, about a week ago. Her parents had thought she'd run away with her high school flame, who was a drug addict and a loser. He was always trying

142

to get her to use her powers for his benefit. You know," he said, wriggling his fingers in the air, a gesture Nik took to mean "magic," "hypnotizing drug dealers to give them all their drugs without paying for them so he could then turn around and sell them, or hypnotizing bank tellers to give them all the cash in the drawer or the manager to give them the code to the safe."

"He gets it," Chang said tersely.

"Okay, so," Nick went on quickly, flushing. "What we're thinking is that the doppelgänger must have either had prior knowledge of our girl here and sought her out specifically for her specialty, or it just got lucky by being in the right place at the right time."

Somehow, Nik doubted it had just gotten lucky. This thing was cunning. It was totally the type to plan things out in advance.

So what did it want with a witch who had specialized in hypnosis, of all things?

"That's just all speculation," Nick amended, turning even redder and running a hand through his hair. Was it the kid's first day on the job?

"So who's the girl in my dungeon?" Nik said gruffly.

"Human, so far as we can tell," Chang said. "We're still waiting on a fingerprint match in our database and are performing other tests in the meantime. Doppelgänger possession has a way of screwing with one's natural signature."

No shit. "Is this all you have to show me?"

"Well—"

"I gotta take a leak," Nik said brusquely, turning to walk away. Actually, he was fine. He was just overstuffed from their bullshit. Though the details of the witch in the woods were interesting, he found them irrelevant at this point.

What did it all mean? What the fuck was he missing?

Agent Chang grabbed hold of his arm. "Hold on a second. We need to show you something else."

"It can wait!" Nik snarled, jerking free and rounding on the man.

To his credit, he didn't flinch as Nik loomed over him, though Nick looked ready to shit his pants. "Word of advice?" Nik said, leaning in with eyes glowing gold. "Don't grab a werewolf. Especially an Alpha. Ever. Got it?"

He turned and stalked off before they could stop him.

Not that they could. He wouldn't advise it, anyway. He wouldn't be held responsible if someone all of a sudden was missing a limb, and somehow, he doubted their health insurance covered "werewolf mauling."

Or maybe it did. Hell if he knew. It was the DPI, the most secretive bunch of motherfuckers he'd ever met.

His feet automatically carried him toward the manor. The early-morning air was crisp; he filled his lungs with the stuff, relishing the freshness of dawn. The night had a way of washing away all the humidity, pollen, and dust that accumulated through the day.

And not that he couldn't appreciate sunlight, but damn was it getting on his nerves this fine morning. Brilliant yellow beams cut through the tree branches, dappling the forest floor and spilling right into his eyes.

As he walked, the ball of worries he'd buried at the back of his mind began to unravel. He wanted to shove them all back, go to sleep, and forget about them. But he knew he'd only be procrastinating because there was so much shit to do, and it sometimes seemed an impossible task to see to everything.

Knowing starting was the hardest part of the battle, he gritted his teeth and decided to tackle what he could.

Starting with how the hell his border patrol had let that thing onto their land in the first place. The stench of Black Magic alone should have given it away.

He reached out with his mind to the farthest reaches of their property.

Perimeter one, check in.

He kept walking, waiting, and at last stopped when there was no response. He repeated himself and again got the silent treatment.

"The fuck?" he muttered, anger prickling just under his skin. Someone was about to get a first-class beating if he didn't hear from them soon.

Perimeter two, check in.

Nothing.

The last command was more growls than intelligible words. *Perimeter three, goddammit, you'd better fucking say something back.*

Silence.

Son of a bitch.

Nik closed his eyes and concentrated on the signatures of his crew. He'd always had excellent memory when it came to sensing his pack's paranormal signatures. It was a skill he'd regrettably developed when Malachite had been ruler. Since keeping Gage safe had been his number-one priority, he'd liked to know where his asshole of an Alpha was at all times. The more he'd focused on it, the stronger that skill had gotten. Now, he could usually pick up where his pack was if he opened his senses wide enough. It was a skill he'd thought about capitalizing on, by way of teaching other werewolves to do it… if only he could find the fucking time.

Throwing his senses wide open, he let the sounds of the forest, the DPI screwing around in his woods, and the distant highway traffic fade away.

With his breathing slow and deep, he focused solely on finding his guards.

A deep frown stamped itself onto his mouth, and his eyes flew open. "Son of a bitch."

They weren't even on duty.

With a growl tearing from his throat, he stormed toward the manor, plowing open the doors and stalking past nervous wolves as he made his way to the lower level.

Being composed mostly of men, the manor had a pretty large-sized man cave on its lowest floor. Located next to the gym, it was complete with wood-paneled walls, arcade games, several leather couches facing a projector TV, the latest versions of the Wii, Xbox, and PlayStation, shelves of movies and video games, a fully stocked bar, a bitching stereo system with surround sound, and, of course, pool tables. It was, undoubtedly, the most popular room in the manor. Before Gage had taken over, this whole area had been a second dungeon. Malachite had had it built when the first cellblock had become overcrowded. While admitting the practicality of having at least one place to hold misfits, Gage had torn out the second dungeon and started construction on a man cave. It had been finished shortly after Nik became Alpha.

Loud classic rock threatened to scramble his brain as he stormed into the room. There they were, the Moonstruck Pack's finest, all gathered around several pool tables or camped out in front of the TV, stupid drunk.

"What the fuck is this?" Nik demanded.

They all looked up. Some scrambled to their feet, but for the most part they looked as if they didn't give two shits that their Alpha was pissed off and standing in the doorway.

"Looks to me like we're playing pool or watching some tube."

Nik's golden eyes flashed to the source of the smartass comment.

That cocky Southern drawl should have been enough to tip him off to who the commenter was.

Ralph Hixon. Accomplished hunter. About sixty years old but in great shape. Always wore plaid button downs, jeans, boots, and his John Deere baseball cap. He'd been a part of the Moonstruck Pack before Malachite had ever taken over and had been a werewolf longer than Nik had been alive. He knew the woods inside and out, often slept out there on the forest floor. Unlike the rest of the perimeter crew, who carried handguns, Ralph favored an old Marlin 336 rifle he'd kept since his hunting days. Said his father had given it to him, whose father had bought it for him as his first rifle when he was a boy and blah, blah, blah. It was one of *those* things. Ralph was emotionally attached to the damn gun, an *object*. As if Nik could talk. He fucking loved the shit out of his cheap-ass Wal-Mart grill, even with Alara subtly hinting that he could do better. Buy a more expensive grill? Yeah. Would it be better? Not necessarily. Not in Nik's book.

Nik walked farther into the room, leveling all of them with a glare that blazed hotter than the surface of the sun. "All of you should be out on patrol right now."

"But the DPI's here," piped up someone from the couch. On the TV, Gerard Butler roared, "Tonight, we dine in hell!"

"So?" Nik said. "Just because the DPI is here doesn't mean any of you can slack off your jobs. This is still our territory, and we still have a pack to defend. Speaking of which, I want to know how that thing got through our lines."

"Hell if we know," Ralph said. "Not like any of us have ever come across a doppelgänger before."

"You should have smelled it. Sensed its signature."

"Well, we didn't."

"Really?" Nik said dryly. "None of you noticed a damn thing was wrong?"

They all stared at him.

The inkling that something wasn't right tickled his brain, but he swatted it aside. His crew was good. He'd hand chosen each one of these men because of their prowess in the woods. Nothing had ever gotten past them before.

So why now?

The mystery of the doppelgänger felt like one gigantic puzzle he couldn't figure out.

Nik's jaw clenched, his gums aching. "Get back outside. Now."

"Why bother?" Ralph said, a challenge in his eyes. "It's not like the DPI's incompetent. They can look after the perimeter for a while."

Nik lost it. He didn't even have to think about it; he just summoned his power, his right as Alpha, to command the pack as he chose. Eyes ablaze with golden power, he said in a low voice, "All of you will go to your posts immediately and report back to me every hour, on the hour."

The spines of every wolf in that room went rigid. More than one glare was thrown his way as they begrudgingly left the room, unable to resist their Alpha's command.

Ralph was the last out. "Maybe there's a little Malachite in you, after all," he said over his shoulder. Murder shone in his eyes. Just before he turned his head, Nik swore he saw Ralph's eyes flash silver, and then he was gone.

Once alone, with nothing but the silence to hear him, Nik sighed long and hard. His shoulders slumped forward, his head hung. He felt... broken. This job, this pack, these people—they were all sucking the life out of him.

Since when has a Johnson been such a pussy?

He could hear his father's voice in his head, loud and clear. *No son of mine is going to be a pussy. You go out there, and you fight. Don't come home 'til you've beaten the shit out of that little snot down the road.* The little snot being the neighbor's boy who'd, along with his friends, been destroying what meager corn crops they'd had. One day, when Nik was a teen, they'd ganged up on him on his way home from school. Well, detention. Same thing to Nik.

Nik hadn't had a problem fighting back. In fact, he'd reveled in it. Still did, he supposed. But when one kid put a gun to his forehead, everything had changed.

He'd been scared shitless. All of a sudden, the possibility that he could die, that he could not be there to protect Gage, became very real. So he'd tucked tail and run on home after the beating. His father had found him in the kitchen, trying to wash the blood off his face and hands. Nik hadn't expected hugs. He'd given up on that fantasy when he was six. And he honestly hadn't been surprised when his father delivered those character-defining words.

Don't be a pussy.

He'd left, gone back down the road, and finished what they'd started, even managing to steal the kid's gun. Nik's story of his first gun wasn't as sentimental as Ralph's.

"Don't be a pussy," Nik muttered aloud and walked out of the room.

The men he'd just sent back into the woods were nowhere near, their signatures growing more distant the farther they walked.

Well, at least that was one less thing to worry about.

Except the fact that they'd been so nonchalant about their duties worried him even more. He wasn't psychic by any means, but he sensed some hardcore discipline in their futures.

Almost as an afterthought—which made him feel guilty as hell, because the witch had been so nice to them—he checked in with the doctor to see how Penelope was faring. Heath informed him that she'd taken off at first light in order to report what had happened to her Council.

Fair enough. He could respect someone who liked to get shit done. Though he still didn't think she should be going poof or vanishing or whatever it was she did after what she'd endured the night before.

Ah, to hell with it. He was no damn doctor. And he didn't have the luxury of worrying about her, ally or no. Penelope was a big witch, and she could take care of herself.

Deciding to check on Alara before resigning himself to his office and the pile of paperwork waiting for him there, Nik bounded up the stairs and walked to their bedroom.

Two fresh guards stood outside their door. Neither of them looked older than twenty, but they were built like linebackers. They'd joined the pack right after Nik took control.

One of them, a lad with dark skin, deep brown eyes, and jet-black hair, stepped in Nik's path. "The Alpha Queen is sleeping," he said, staring Nik down. Even in his Green Hornet T-shirt, he looked intimidating—for any-one but Nik, who stared at him.

"Do you see who's standing in front of you?"

"Yes." A split-second flash of silver.

Nik blinked several times. He needed his eyes checked. Tired as hell from all this bullshit, and tired as hell in gen-eral, he said, "Let me pass."

"No."

His jaw actually dropped. "No?"

"No. You cannot enter." The other guard came to stand beside him, as if to give his buddy backup. Both of them stood there and stared at him, big arms crossed over their big chests.

Pushed past his limit, Nik growled, "Get out of my way." He flung his compulsion at them, a direct order from the Alpha. Gage had always been too noble to use his right to command them. Nik, on the other hand, wasn't afraid to hurt feelings and bust skulls to get something done, especially not where the well-being of his mate was concerned.

Though they resisted, the two moved aside, and Nik brushed past them.

He stopped.

Alara wasn't in bed. And her signature wasn't there.

"Alara?" he called, checking the room, just to be sure. He was so out of it today, he might be hallucinating that her signature was gone. He looked everywhere, even stupid places like the closet, the shower—hell, even under the bed.

Nope. His mate was really fucking gone.

On the verge of panic, he was about to shout for the guards when he spied a note sitting on the bed. The paper was nearly the same color as their comforter, hiding it from his view the first time he'd searched the bed.

His eyes flew over the neat script he knew to be his mate's.

Couldn't sleep. Gone for a walk to clear my head. Don't worry, babe. Will be back. Love, Alara

First of all, she never called him "babe." Like, ever.

"Lord Alpha." Another wolf under his command stood at the open door. "There's been a disturbance."

Son of a bitch, did this never end?

He was already walking toward the door. "Where?"

"The garage. Old Man Wayne was attacked."

Nik's brows furrowed. Wayne was as sweet as old men came. In the years Nik had known him, he'd come to think of him as a grandpa. If someone had hurt him...

But his concern over Wayne paled next to his concern for his mate.

Where are you, Alara?

He wasn't going to bother asking Tweedledee and Tweedledum outside their bedroom door if they'd heard anything. Since they'd kept insisting she'd been asleep, he figured they couldn't have much more to offer in the way of information.

It didn't take long to get to the garage. Wayne sat on a stool, rubbing his head.

Nik approached him. "What happened?" he asked gently.

"I... I don't remember," Wayne said, sounding baffled. "One minute I was monitoring the cameras, and the next, I was waking up with a splitting headache!"

"Easy," Nik murmured, looking around. Well, fuck. Someone had done a number on their equipment. Yeah, he'd smelled the smoke and burning electrical cords from outside the garage, but he'd been more focused on making sure a member of his pack was all right. At any rate, he wasn't happy about the roasted equipment.

"Anything missing?" he asked.

"Um, that blue Subaru BRZ."

Nik paused. Of all the sweet rides in their garage, why the hell would someone steal that? It was a nice car, yeah, but compared to the Ferrari F12berlinetta...

A glint of gold from the floor, underneath the desk where Wayne had fallen, caught Nik's eye. Bending over, he retrieved the item.

His breath stuck in his throat.

It was Alara's pinky ring. *It's a stupid piece of plastic,* she said in his memory, showing it off to him when he'd asked. *Izzy won it for me at a fair. I wear it to keep her close to me, I suppose.*

Alara had been here. She never took that ring off, not ever.

Realization slowly dawned on him. "I need to go," he said, grabbing a set of keys from the wall and walking into the garage.

"Where?" a guard asked, following.

Nik unlocked the silver Porsche Panamera and climbed inside. "Don't know. There's something I need to do. See to it that Wayne gets seen by Heath."

He closed the door and turned the engine, gunning it out of the garage and leaving the guy staring after him, scratching his head.

Alara hadn't gone on a walk. She'd been taken or forced to go against her will.

Otherwise, why deliberately leave the ring for him to find?

It occurred to Nik that he should probably call for backup, but he decided against it. Gage had his own problems as His-Royal-Importantness. Plus, it would take him too long to get there. Sure, he could probably order one of his witches to beam him or poof him there. But Nik didn't want to be a nuisance. He could handle this problem on his own. Nik smirked. Let his little brother sort out the rest of the werewolf nation's issues.

His pack couldn't be trusted. They'd made that abundantly clear in the events of these past few hours. Slacking on the job, pigheadedness, unreliability… things weren't boding well for the Moonstruck Pack.

And that weird gleam in their eyes… he didn't know if he was seeing things or if there really was something more to that.

Either way, he didn't have time to get to the bottom of that now. He had to find his mate. Something was clearly wrong with her, and he would never in a million years leave her in jeopardy. He wouldn't deserve a mate, or have the right to be called an Alpha, if he let something happen to her. He was barely able to keep the pack together as it was. The thought of someone new taking over just because his mate was killed—

Don't think that way. Don't fucking think that way.

She wasn't dead, wasn't going to die, dammit. Not if he could help it.

The Porsche's tires squealed as he slid onto the highway and slammed his foot down on the gas.

It would be wise to let someone know where he was, just in case something happened. Reaching out to his Beta, Jared, through their pack-bond, he informed him of what he was driving and the direction he was going in. Alara's signature was faint, meaning she was way ahead of him but not so far that he couldn't tell the direction she'd gone.

Nik told Jared he'd contact him once he found what he was looking for and told him to keep an eye on everyone.

After Jared assured his Alpha he would do his best, Nik allowed himself to focus on the open road.

The silvery eyes, the doppelgänger, the DPI, Ralph—none of it mattered.

Right now, the most important thing on his mind was finding his mate.

CHAPTER THIRTEEN

ABOUT FIFTEEN MINUTES INTO THE DRIVE, THE doppelgänger had Alara get onto the interstate. Alara tried not to let her nerves show as she drove south, heading toward Texas. Her pinky felt empty without her sister's ring, and it took all her focus not to consciously think about leaving it behind.

Had Nik found it yet?

Dropping it on the floor while the doppelgänger was distracted had been an afterthought, something that hadn't occurred to her until they'd gotten ready to leave. Alara had kept the doppelgänger busy chatting. If it had noticed anything amiss, it hadn't said.

She deeply hoped Nik would come, a secret wish she didn't dare give thought or voice to. It wasn't so much about him rescuing her as it was not trusting the doppelgänger to keep her body safe. With him around, it was more likely to be careful.

She hoped.

And if it tried to turn on Nik, Alara would fight back with everything she had in her. It wouldn't be allowed to hurt her beloved. She just hoped that if it came down to that, she would be strong enough in spirit to defend her will.

Turn here, exit thirty-four, said the doppelgänger.

Alara put her blinker on and got off the interstate.

Go to the right, toward Crossroads.

She did as the doppelgänger said, knowing it was useless to ask questions and that there was no point in resisting much right now. The doppelgänger had made it clear it would take control if need be, and Alara didn't want to inadvertently ram into a light pole or end up in a ditch because of an internal power struggle. The police would think she was crazy, drunk, high, maybe all three. Getting thrown in jail was not part of her escape plan.

Alara had never been to this part of the state before. In general, her father hadn't bothered much with small, rural towns, preferring to conduct his business and place his focus on the larger cities throughout the US. Every now and then he would deign to visit a small town, but it was always just for show. Usually, a film crew was nearby, and within the month, pictures and video clips of the gracious High King of Werewolves would trickle into the Underworld media system. Usually with some fluff piece about him funding a local charity or helping to bring commerce to poorer cities. The display, the insincerity of it all, had disgusted Alara.

The town of Crossroads was literally just down the

road, at a major intersection of different highways. A large green sign read, Welcome to Crossroads, home of the Crossroads Pirates. Population 7,000, Census 2011.

It was nice; the whole town was older but looked well kept. It looked like an industrial city, specializing in food-product manufacturing. Several gray structures Alara knew to be plants coughed up smoke in the distance, just outside of town.

The doppelgänger acted as her GPS as she drove through the town square, eventually following one of the back roads out to the countryside. Cornstalks sprang up all around, swaying in the breeze. Verdant fields speckled with grazing cattle stretched out into the horizon on either side of the road. Sunlight beat through the windshield, warming the car and Alara's skin. She cranked the AC up a bit higher, turning the temperature down as low as it would go.

You see that plant coming up, the large light-gray one on the left? the doppelgänger said.

Yes?

That's where we're going. But we're not going to park there. We're going to pull over at this gas station up the road, park, and walk to the plant.

About a quarter of a mile away from the plant, a tiny BP sat. Its sign was yellow, the green long faded due to overexposure to the sun and the elements.

Alara's stomach churned. Putting on her blinker, she turned into the BP and parked along the side of the store as the doppelgänger instructed.

To avoid security cameras, it said as she got out and

locked the car up.

She set out on foot back in the direction she came, jogging along the highway briefly before ducking into one of the cornfields for better coverage.

Having been exercising regularly for a while now, thanks to her mother's relentless commentary about her weight, Alara was used to running. It felt good, feeding more energy into her body and giving her something to focus on, other than the fact that this was surely a bad idea.

As she ran, she took inventory of her surroundings. A dirt path cut through the cornfield, about a quarter of a mile to her left. When she neared the edge of the cornfield, she knelt and quietly observed.

The plant had two main buildings from which smoke billowed, high and fluffy, into the sky. A few other buildings sat alongside them, some connecting to the main structure and some not. A brick sign with a colorful plaque reading CHARLIE'S CHICKEN sat at the end of the driveway, in case the twenty-foot emblem stamped to the main building facing the road was somehow missed.

A parking lot, about half full, stretched alongside the largest building. The six-foot chain-link fence surrounding the property almost made it feel like a detention facility.

Facing them on the side of the largest building was a door with some keypad device meant for swiping a security badge. Above the door, the narrow shape of a security camera loomed. A mountain of a man stood beside the door, dressed head to toe in black and looking more like a mercenary than a security guard. He had a meanness about his eyes that made Alara shiver. The hem of his shirt lifted around his hip—he had a gun.

Out of habit, she scanned his signature, checking to see if he was supernatural or human.

A frown formed. *That's a werewolf.*

Yes.

What's a werewolf doing in a place like this?

You'll see.

More riddles and few answers.

Well, now what? Alara asked the doppelgänger.

We break in, it said simply.

Break in, Alara stated flatly. *All to steal a dagger. Why? I know you said it will stop Mistress Black, but how?*

If I bothered to explain the intricacies of the spell I have in mind, we'd be here all day. Just trust me.

Her teeth gritted. It looked as if she wasn't going to get any more out of the doppelgänger.

Alara had never been good with blind trust. It had often gotten her bitten.

She glanced over her shoulder, back in the direction of the highway. It would do her no good, running. The doppelgänger would only fight her the whole way and, with her being as exhausted as she was, inevitably seize control.

Turning back to the facility, she said, *How do we break in?*

Just walk up to the door.

Aren't you worried about the guard?

No.

Silence.

Growling a sigh, Alara checked to make sure the

sidewalk leading up to the entrance was clear before swallowing her fear and stepping out of the cornfield. The doppelgänger briefly took over. Alara's fingertips briefly tingled with magic, and she flexed her hand.

For the security camera, the doppelgänger said. *The footage of the guard alone should start to loop, though it won't last forever. We'll need to be in and out quickly.*

No problem. Alara didn't want to stay here any longer than she had to.

The werewolf immediately zeroed in on her as she approached. His eyes swept her down and up, and his face scrunched up in confusion. "You can't be here," he said in a deep bass.

Act lost, the doppelgänger hissed. *And don't fight me if you want to live.*

Alara gulped. Her smile had no problem being zany, thanks to her nerves. "Is this the Tyson plant? I'm here for a job interview."

He looked pointedly at the sign that clearly said CHARLIE'S CHICKEN and then back to her. "No," he said slowly, clearly thinking he was dealing with an idiot. His eyes narrowed. "Aren't you a little underdressed for a job interview?"

"Oh, this isn't Tyson's?" Alara said, ignoring the comment about her attire as she sidled up to him. She stomped her foot. "Google Maps lied to me again!"

The guard sniffed. A low growl rumbled in his throat. "You're a wolf."

"Hmmm?"

"We don't hire outside wolves. Ever." He started to

reach for his gun, the other hand going for the walkie-talkie at his side.

Alara's body leapt into motion, the doppelgänger seizing control quicker than she could react. The ball of her foot connected with the man's hand, making him drop the gun. He gaped at her, stunned. She summoned a blast of dark power, and her fist shot out, clipping his temple with a magic-packed punch. The guard's eyes rolled back as he fell to the ground, out cold.

Once again, Alara was speechless as the doppelgänger directed her body. She knelt and picked up the gun, tucking it into the waistband of her pants, and grabbed the walkie-talkie. A wave of dizziness flowed through her, and she swayed, grabbing her head and holding it until the world stilled.

The fatigue will pass, the doppelgänger murmured, all business, as Alara grabbed the man's badge. After dragging the body into the cornfield, which felt like trying to drag an elephant, Alara swiped the badge and entered the building.

What about the cameras in here?

Allow me. Power surged up from Alara's mind as her lips moved against her will, uttering words in that strange, beautiful language she did not know. Her knees shook when the enchantment was completed, and she propped a hand along the wall to steady herself.

What did you do? Alara rasped.

Made us invisible to the eyes of mortals and cameras. Magic can still detect us. We'll have to be discreet.

No kidding? Alara said dryly. As if breaking and

entering didn't require discretion.

The inside was fairly drab, with white walls and concrete flooring. There were no decorations, not even a potted plant. Fluorescent lighting lit the way as she walked quickly down the hallway, keeping one hand on the wall until the weakness passed. She opened her senses wide, checking for more paranormal signatures, but felt none.

How do you know so much about fighting? she asked the doppelgänger. *And magic?*

I know so much about magic because I've been in the heads of some of the greatest warlocks and witches the world has ever seen. Though Black Magic is inherent for most doppelgängers. We were born of it.

Because you're evil, Alara wanted to say but kept her mental mouth shut. *What about fighting?*

The same, it said, as if shrugging. *You pick up an assortment of useful knowledge when you head hop.*

You mean body hop.

It was silent a beat. The sweet prickle of anger kissed her veins. Alara, frankly, didn't care if she'd pissed it off. She'd never forgive it for what it was doing to her right now. Putting her in danger, taking control as if she were merely a machine for the doppelgänger to use as it pleased.

Not for long. Alara had made it a promise, that she would never give up trying to expel it, and she damn well intended to keep it.

The forever-long hallway eventually ended in a fork. On the wall at the end of the hallway hung a sign, with arrows pointing in either direction. Production Room and Storage to the left and Offices, Break Room, and

Restrooms to the right.

Take a left, the doppelgänger snapped.

Alara smirked a little. Guess it really didn't like being called a body snatcher.

The urge to needle the doppelgänger further almost took hold, but she stopped herself. It was childish and wouldn't solve her problem, no matter how much fun it sounded like.

The left turn had led to another secured-access steel door. Swiping her badge, she hefted the door open. It was a locker room, gray as deep winter and just as cold.

Thank God she was a werewolf. If her body temperature wasn't naturally higher, she might find it unbearable to work here. As it was, she didn't see how humans could stand it.

Checking for signatures of life and finding the place empty, she stepped into the room and her shoulders relaxed.

Find a uniform to change into, ordered the doppelgänger. *And a mask. Tie your hair up, and put it under the cap.*

Alara started sifting through lockers. None of them had locks. Apparently, this place had a high-trust code Alara found unbelievable. Or perhaps that was her inner cynic peeping its head out.

After raiding a few lockers, she found a long-sleeved white lab coat, a red plastic apron with the logo CHARLIE'S CHICKEN over the left breast, long, red latex gloves, a surgical mask, and a red latex hair cap.

After throwing all that on over her clothes, she crossed

to the other side of the room and swiped the badge against the security panel. A second steel door clicked open, and cool mist floated out.

A decontamination room, the doppelgänger said. *To detect traces of rogue magic.*

Alara hesitated on the threshold. *Will we set it off?*

No. Allow me to worry about it.

Holding her breath, Alara crossed into the small room. The door clicked shut, and blue-and-purple mist shot out of nozzles on the walls. The sparkling vapors wrapped around her, circling her, searching her body for unwanted elements. Alara guessed she'd passed the test when the mist was sucked back into the nozzles in a blink, and the stoplight-looking thing above the exit switched from red to green.

Go through that door, the doppelgänger said. *And prepare yourself.*

Prepare myself for what? She swiped her badge and opened the door.

A blast of cool air that reeked of grease and blood slammed into her, nearly making her gag. The stink seemed to stick to her throat, making it harder to breathe. *Oh God! You should've said not to breathe!*

Focus, the doppelgänger said, though the strain in its voice suggested it was having just as hard a time with the odor as Alara was.

As Alara tried to force back the rising bile, she stared out over the main production room, a maze of bloodied conveyor belts, glistening, silvery blades, and red-stained water leaking into large drains.

One thing became crystal clear.

This isn't a chicken processing plant, Alara said.

Actually, it is, said the doppelgänger, *but it's a cover for an illegal magic operation.*

Getting her A game on, Alara steeled her brain and sniffed. Another wave of toxic grease and rank blood assaulted her nose, but she sifted through those smells. There was an undercurrent of something else, something that burned, like chlorine. *I've never smelled anything like it,* she said, growling in frustration. *I can't tell what it is.*

If you could, then you wouldn't be the proper lady I thought you to be.

Huh? Did the doppelgänger just tease her?

It's mostly potions, the doppelgänger went on, answering the question that had been on the tip of Alara's tongue. *Love spells, poisons, enchantments… You name it, they make it.*

And sell it all on the Black Market. It kind of went without saying, but Alara felt the need to say it aloud anyway.

Workers milled about the floor, all weighed down by the same bulky ensemble Alara wore. It looked as if there were two halves of the factory. On the left side was the chicken-processing operation, while the production line on the right handled the magic. As Alara watched the glistening bottles of potions *whiz* by, they started to flicker, looking like chicken.

It's an illusion only paranormals can see through, the doppelgänger said. *Which is why, as you'll notice, all the workers are human.*

Alara refocused on the workers. The doppelgänger

was right; not a single paranormal in here. *I'll bet the staff is paranormal.*

You'll bet correctly. You see those stairs on your left? Take them down to the ground floor.

You couldn't miss the stairs; they were bright red and metal. A good thing, actually, Alara thought as she climbed down them. A new worker—or an intruder, such as herself—might not know where the exits were, and these stuck out like a neon-green house in an upper-class suburban neighborhood.

The floor—like, literally, the entire floor—was covered in pink-tinted water. Alara wished she had worn crappier shoes. These boots weren't cheap, and she really didn't want to take bleach to them to get the bloodstains and odors out. As she walked, the bloodied water splashed, leaving little pink bubbles to pop in her wake.

She resisted the urge to wince or go running back to the ladder. These shoes would officially be considered ruined. Even if she bleached them, the stink of blood, decay, and rot would never go away. At least, not for her overly sensitized werewolf nose.

Relax, the doppelgänger snapped. *Or you'll draw attention to us.*

It's a little hard to take it easy when you're walking around in a festering sea of blood, she snapped back. Her mood was quickly dissolving.

Alara's eyes wandered over to the production line. Workers were stationed every few feet, each silently and robotically performing their duties. One, whose gloves were slick with blood, swore as he dropped a chicken—a real one, not a fake—onto the floor, where it landed with a loud splash. Certain he was going to throw it away, Alara was appalled when he instead scooped it up and placed it back on the conveyor belt. No one around him batted a lash.

Her eyes snapped forward, and she quickened her pace. *I'm going to be sick.*

You're surprised? This sort of thing goes on all the time, especially in an Underworld-only factory, where food sanitation laws aren't monitored as strictly as they should be.

The image of the chicken sitting on her plate, coated in God knew how much bacteria just waiting to wreak havoc on her insides, made her nearly throw up. She needed another topic, anything else. *Where are we going?*

You see that door over there, on the opposite side of the room?

Alara looked. A wooden door with a golden plaque she couldn't read stood beside a window with opened blinds—an office, probably for upper management or the production manager.

Yes, she said.

Go to it.

… Just waltz right in?

You question me a lot, werewolf.

Because you won't tell me any of your motives or what the hell is going on!

Ssshhh… I'll reward your patience and trust. I swear.

Alara had serious doubts about that. Her jaw ticked as she walked, which turned into more of a stomp because her anger was riding so high.

Turning the corner, Alara drew up abruptly.

A guard was approaching. Clad all in black as the guy outside had been, and possibly sporting even larger muscles and a meaner leer, he prowled across the floor. His slitted eyes carefully observed the workers, watching for any sign of trouble. A handgun sat freely exposed in the holster strapped to his waist. The tingling sensation that heralded another paranormal danced along Alara's tendons. Also like the guard outside, this man was a werewolf.

And he was heading right toward her.

Alara's step faltered.

Keep going, the doppelgänger urged.

But he's a were. He'll be able to sense me. And stop her or, more likely, shoot her.

I'll hide your signature.

Like you did for that girl in our dungeon? Alara said accusingly.

Maybe. Maybe not. Perhaps she was simply human.

More secrets. She nibbled her lip. *I'm going to call you Secret,* Alara announced. *Because I need something to call you.* Her mother, in one of her few motherly moments, had told Alara that if you can name a demon of yours, you can overcome it. She'd been referring to Alara's weight and her food addiction—anything covered in chocolate, dipped in caramel, or fried in butter, essentially—but Alara figured it would work just as well for the doppelgänger.

A raspy, amused laugh. *An appropriate name indeed. Very well. I shall henceforth be known as Secret.*

Alara darkly smiled. *Name the demon. Then you can destroy it,* her mother had said. Sage, deadly words she would keep buried deep within her until the time was right to strike.

The guard approached, less than a foot away now, and Alara's shoulders tensed up near her ears. Keeping her eyes down, she ducked beside him as he passed, not even casting her a cursory glance.

She exhaled a long breath. *That was close—*

"Hey."

The bark made her jump. Slowly turning around, she saw that the guard had stopped and was staring at her. His gaze swept her over from head to toe, as if trying to place her.

"You have on the wrong footwear," he said, frowning at her soaked boots. "And you're not wearing any footies."

Footies? She looked at the worker closest to her. Sure enough, he wore red latex footies over his shoes.

Damn. How had she missed that?

"Sorry," she blurted. "I'm new."

"Thought you didn't look familiar." Another deep frown, this time laced with suspicion. "Let me see your ID."

Oh God. "I…"

Take out the badge! Secret hissed.

With her brain too scrambled by exhaustion and fear to argue, Alara fumbled for the badge stashed in her pocket and thrust it toward the man. He snatched it up, glaring at the piece of plastic as if trying to see through it. "Maria Martinez," he growled.

"Huh?" Secret gave her the internal equivalent of elbowing her in the ribs. "Oh, yes!"

Still frowning, he searched her face, as if he was attempting to match up the picture on the badge, which was of a woman Alara had never seen before, with the woman standing in front of him.

At last, he handed back the badge. "You're supposed to keep your badge visible at all times," he said sternly. "And grab some footies before you ruin your shoes."

The touch of concern was unexpected from a man like him. She'd half expected him to rip her a new one, drill sergeant style, for her carelessness. "Um, I will. Thank you, sir."

His mouth twitched in a smile, and he returned to patrolling the floor.

OhmyGod, ohmyGod, ohmyGod kept replaying in her head as her knees shook. Whether it was from fear or from the magic Secret had obviously woven to distort the badge, she couldn't be sure.

Nicely done, Secret said, all business.

You're going to be the death of me, Alara squeaked, her voice high pitched from terror.

As I said, I won't allow any harm to come to you. Go to the office, quickly, before he comes back or someone else discovers us.

Alara wasted no time. She hightailed it across the production room and to the office. The name on the plaque by the door was unfamiliar—Simon Peters. Peering through the blinds to find no one inside, she tried the doorknob.

It was locked.

More muttered words she couldn't pronounce, and two seconds later, the door opened.

Alara glanced over her shoulder to make sure no one was watching. The guard was focused on another poor soul at the other end of the room, and all the workers' eyes were trained on their jobs. Slipping inside, she closed the door and relocked it. *Now what?*

Now we wait.

Wait? For what?

More like for whom.

The office was decorated plainly, with a fake potted plant wrapped up in white twinkle lights, an oak desk, neatly organized office supplies in the cabinet to the left, and a single picture framing a seascape at sunrise.

Pull your gun, Secret said. *Disarm the safety.*

I know how to use a gun! Alara snapped, pulling out the weapon she'd lifted off the first guard. She wondered if he'd been discovered missing yet. If not, her luck couldn't hold out for much longer. Surely, the guards did a security check where they touched base with one another. When he didn't respond…

Her heart beat that much faster, a feat Alara hadn't thought possible. Good God, this whole nightmare was going to give her a heart attack. Suddenly, the peace and boredom of pack life back at Crescent Manor seemed blissful, like Heaven, even.

Footsteps approached, dress shoes.

The manager must be coming.

Hide behind the door, Secret said.

Alara tucked herself against the wall adjacent to the door, the gun clutched to her chest.

Her heart beat harder, thumping against her sternum

and making her whole body shake. Blood rushed through her veins, carrying her pulse to her ears, until it momentarily drowned out all other sound.

The approaching footsteps grew louder, along with a heated argument. "I don't care how impatient Mistress Black is," he growled. "Tell her I'll get her her money when I have it! We're behind in production."

This plant belongs to Mistress Black? Alara asked.

Sssh!

Her breath seemed twice as loud in the moment before the man jammed his key in the lock and opened the door.

Alara bit her lip and stopped breathing altogether.

The door shut, and a tall, dark-haired man wearing a black business suit strutted in. His signature crackled with power—a Red Warlock. The phone was still held up to his ear. "Did you not hear what I just said?" Pause. "Yes, I'm aware of what happens to people who don't pay her back." Another pause, accompanied by a swipe of his brow. Sweat came back on his hand.

With a growl, he hung up on whoever was still snapping at him and cursed, tossing the cell phone on his desk. Walking around to the other side of his desk, he sank down into his chair with a long sigh—and looked straight at her.

CHAPTER FOURTEEN

THE SENSATION OF HER ARM GRACEFULLY UNFOLDING to point the gun at the stranger's head was surreal.

Her body but not her doing. Which created a huge disconnect in her mind. As though if she bit her lip, blinked really hard, or pinched her arm, she would wake up back home, with Nik asleep beside her. She would watch him sleep, poke the little air bubble in his cheek caused by his snoring, and then smile and shake her head that nothing could wake him when he was out cold. She'd roll over, he'd mumble something, and those big, strong arms of his would wrap around her waist and pull her close.

It sounded wonderful. She yearned for that simple life, not the twisting, never-ending nightmare she now lived.

"Don't move," Secret said, using Alara's mouth. Her voice was still her own. She had that, at least.

Blue eyes flecked with embers stared back at her. The stranger's face was handsome, for an older man. A few wrinkles striped his forehead and around the contours of his mouth and eyes, and his dark-brown hair was streaked with gray. He had a stern set to his bearded jaw and a hardness about his eyes that suggested he was not a man to toy with.

The shock on his face mirrored her own.

Who is he? Alara snapped at Secret. *Dammit, you made me point a gun at this man's head. If we're resorting to murder now, you'd better start giving me some answers!*

He's a high-ranking official of the Order, Mistress Black's coven. He's the one who ordered Gerard to kill your family.

The floor dropped out from under her. The quake of shock that rocked her body might have sent her to her knees had Secret not kept her standing.

"Oh God," she rasped aloud, barely able to siphon enough air into her lungs to speak. It felt as if her lungs had stopped working, along with her brain.

Simon's dark brows stooped in confusion.

Alara waited for the anger to hit, to drive her to pull the trigger.

Pop! The sound of the bullet tearing his brain to shreds.

Bam! The sound of his lifeless body hitting the floor.

Those were the sounds of revenge.

She pictured killing him over and over in her head, tried imagining the satisfaction of avenging her family's deaths.

…It wouldn't come. The relief from anger, the ache of despair.

And that was when she knew that no matter how

many people she killed, no matter the reason, it would never bring her family back. They were gone, forever. And no amount of bloodshed would ever resurrect them.

Tears flooded her eyes, making her face hot.

Alara's brain locked up as she stared back at Simon. How was she supposed to feel, staring at the face of her family's executioner? Scared? Shocked? Betrayed? Enraged?

After a few more seconds of shell-shocked silence, the surprise on his face faded, and he composed himself. He cocked that handsome head to the side, studying her face, as if trying to place her. Realization lit up his eyes. "Alara Crescent," he said, his deep voice raspy. The strong stink of cigarettes clinging to his pores told her why. "Or is it Johnson now? Congratulations, by the way." He started to rise.

"The safety's off, just so you know," Secret said. Again, her voice, but ten times more threatening. "Sit down."

He obeyed, carefully sinking back into the chair. Those blue eyes never blinked as he watched her, a small smirk propped up on his mouth. "How did you find me?" Those long, elegant hands folded themselves in his lap, as if this were a casual meet and greet and she didn't have a gun pointed at his head. "Well? How did you sniff me out?" The smirk broke into a grin.

Sniff him out, indeed.

Alara's annoyance grew. Cocky bastard. He meant for his ease to scare her. *Tough shit,* as Nik would say. This warlock was messing with the wrong wolf, not intimidating her in the least. Thanks to her time at Court, she knew his type well—the men and women whose heads were so swollen from power, wealth, and an inflated sense of self-importance that they thought they owned the world and everyone in it.

"I have my ways." Secret had spoken for her again.

Alara was happy to let it. She couldn't think right now. Her head and heart were only so big, and there were far too many powerful emotions tumbling around inside of her.

Highways of silence stretched between them. "I am sorry for the barbaric way your family was killed," he said at last, sounding anything but. "They weren't supposed to die that way."

"But they were supposed to die. *I* was supposed to die." Secret didn't fight for control; it let her speak.

"Yes," he said without hesitation.

Her mouth formed a hard line, and her eyes turned to ice. "Save your fake apologies for someone who gives a damn." Secret jumped in. "Now, give me the blade."

Simon stiffened, shifting his body to hide something tucked inside his jacket. Alara caught a glimmer of a ruby in the hilt of what appeared to be a dagger.

Alara stared. Something dark and unbidden scraped across the surface of her memory.

There it was, the dagger her father had used to kill her mother. The same dagger Gerard had driven into her baby sister's heart.

She growled, possessed with the sudden urge to rip this man's throat out with her fangs.

We're wasting time, Secret snapped. "The blade, now,"

it said through Alara's mouth.

Though he was still turned away from her in a useless attempt at hiding the dagger, he didn't bother denying he had it. Good. At least he wasn't going to treat her like an idiot.

"What do you need it for?" he asked instead, still not moving.

"That's none of your concern."

He squinted. "What's wrong with your eyes?"

"What do you mean?"

"I saw them…" He shook his head. "Never mind." That tall, graceful body stood. "Alara—"

"Don't come any closer." Alara wanted to back away, not because she was afraid of him but because merely being in the same room with the man responsible for ruining her life was overwhelming. The thought of him coming closer to her was unbearable.

Secret locked up her body as she was about to shrink into the corner, making her hold her ground. Alara's teeth gritted.

Simon froze, both hands in the air. "I never meant for any of this to go this far." Regret briefly flashed through his eyes.

"But it did," Alara bit out. "And you'll have to live with that for the rest of your miserable life, however long that might be." Quickly losing her patience and ready to get the hell out of there and away from him, she said, "Last chance. Give. Me. The. Blade."

He shifted his weight, swallowing hard. Sweat glistened across his weathered brow. "I can't. She'll… she'll kill me…"

"Not if I do it first."

The gun went off.

Time stopped as the bullet fired across the room, straight for Simon's heart.

As Alara watched Simon's imminent death unfold, a black pit of horror opened up in her stomach.

She was going to kill someone. She was officially going to be a murderer. Sure, she'd assisted in the death of her father. Yes, her paws were already partially stained red, but this was different. With this, she'd never get her innocence back.

Oh God. What had Secret done? What had *she* done?

Her quiet moment in the woods with her mate came to mind. *Killing changes you. It blackens your soul, and once you cross that line, you can never turn back.*

She started forward. "No!"

The air directly in front of Simon lit up with flames, a swirling, writhing vortex of fire and tendrils of Red Magic. Simon grunted, both hands braced behind the fire shield as it swallowed the bullet. The flames grew hotter, bluer, until their indigo light literally melted the bullet. With a final cry, Simon threw the shield downward, casting aside the ruined bullet in a puddle of metal.

Alara's jaw dropped.

This was no ordinary Red Warlock. He was supremely powerful, more so than she'd ever suspected. No wonder he had a seat on Mistress Black's inner circle.

Panting hard and deathly pale, Simon lifted his eyes to her. Anger burned there. "You'll regret that," he rasped, right as he launched a fireball at her.

Alara started to duck, but Secret took over, throwing up her hands. A pit of deepest midnight tore open the air in front of her, sucking the fireball inside before blinking out.

Any color left in Simon's face leached out of his skin. "Black Magic? You're a Crescent. There is no dark power in your family's line. How is this possible?"

"Wouldn't you like to know?" Secret said with a wicked smile. With a flick of her wrist, shadows poured out of her fingers. They snaked through the air, wrapping themselves around Simon's head. Choking noises sputtered from the cloud, and he grasped at his throat. The cloud vanished, revealing eyes round with terror. The vibrant blue of his irises, as well as the black dot of his pupils, had been blotted out by a milky white film. As he continued to gasp for air that wouldn't come, he began flailing his arms, almost in a paddling motion.

What did you do to him? Alara demanded, watching in horror.

It's an illusion spell. I made him believe he was drowning—his worst fear, Secret added with a smile in its voice.

You what?

Secret shrugged it off. *You'd be surprised how many Red Witches and Warlocks fear death by water. Grab the dagger while he's distracted.*

Alara scurried across the room, reaching into his jacket and unhooking the dagger strapped at his waist. Her lip curled up at the vile thing. She wondered if her family's blood still coated the blade or if they had had the decency to at least clean it off.

Alara looked at Simon, who still swam toward the ceiling as if trying to escape an ocean of endless depths.

A small smile of dark satisfaction curled her lips as she watched him die.

Good, she thought.

She caught herself, blinking. No. No, she wasn't going to be that kind of girl, that kind of queen. If she allowed that darkness, that anger, to take over, she knew she'd lose herself completely. And she didn't like the idea of who she would become.

Fight, Izzy whispered at the back of her mind.

Let him go, Alara said.

No.

Yes, she pressed, reaching for the magic.

Secret immediately blocked her. *We need to get out of here.*

Not until you release him! It hurt to say it, but it felt right. And she trusted her gut.

Fight, Alara. Don't let the ugliness win, urged Izzy, all innocence and goodness, the light in Alara's darkness.

She had been so much better a person than Alara. Why did she have to die?

"It should have been me," Alara whispered.

Come on! Secret screeched.

An alarm sounded, and red light flashed outside of the office as the sirens wailed.

Secret swore. *They must have found our incapacitated guard. Time to go.*

Footsteps thundered toward the office. The doorknob

rattled but didn't give, right before someone started kicking the door, hard. The reverberations rolled through the floor and into Alara's feet.

Jerking her arms upward, Secret yelled, "*Barium steelio!*" A thick, smoky barrier coalesced in the air in front of the wall containing the door and the window. Outside the office, the security guards pushed past the crowd of workers and began banging against the glass with the butts of their guns, fire extinguishers—whatever they had handy that was hard enough to break glass that had been clearly reinforced and, possibly, enchanted.

That barrier won't last long, Secret said, heading to the desk. *Your body isn't used to magic, and your energy's draining quickly. Search the drawers.*

Alara started ripping open drawers and riffling through them. So far, they were stuffed with only office supplies and documents. *What am I looking for?*

Let me look. I'll be faster.

A loud boom shook the room, followed by the sound of hundreds of glass shards hitting the concrete floor. They'd broken through the window somehow. She didn't dare look up and break Secret's concentration as the angry mob of guards began to beat on the magical barrier Secret had erected.

Come on, come on, Secret muttered, fingers flying. *A warlock this powerful has to keep a stash of—aha!* With a delicate click, Secret pushed a button underneath the top drawer, and a hidden compartment slid out. Alara had no idea what all this stuff was—bottles of shimmering liquid and opaque containers containing who knew what—but

Secret obviously did. Grabbing a small silver pillbox, it dumped a handful of what looked like glistening white pearls into Alara's hand.

What's that going to do? Alara asked.

Save our asses. Close your eyes. Raising her hand, Alara threw the pearls down right as the barrier of magic finally broke.

An explosion of light was released from the pearls the moment they hit the floor, blinding everyone around her and sending a shock wave through the air that knocked them off their feet.

Alara was instantly on the move, guided by the doppelgänger's killer instincts. Jumping onto the desk, Alara gripped the hilt of the blade with her teeth and leapt through the air toward the window. Her body Shifted in midair, and the beautiful umber-colored wolf landed on the cold, concrete floor of the production room. Her paws slipped along the muck; digging in her claws, she found better traction and sprinted toward the exit she'd used to waltz in there.

No! Go to your left! There's another way out!

Veering sharply as gunfire split the water near her, she banked hard and bolted down a hallway. The guards thundered after her, swearing and screaming orders into their walkie-talkies.

Just as Alara was nearing the end of the hallway, a guard burst around the corner, gun aimed for her head.

Give me control! Secret screamed.

Being cornered front and back, Alara didn't question it. Surrendering her senses to the doppelgänger's expertise, she marveled at what followed.

It was a bloodbath, a beautiful, deadly dance between wolf and human. The guard was no match for her superior strength and speed. Ripping out his throat, she turned and clawed another guard, who didn't fare much better. Blood slicked the floor, splashing on the white walls like some abstract painting.

And for a few seconds that would forever vibrate inside Alara as a warning, she relished the bloodlust. It was like being at the gym, a powerful release of anger, pain, and suffering.

Only, with Secret's astonishing knowledge of killing techniques, the revenge she'd only dreamed of was now a crimson reality.

She was a warrior, an angel of death come to wreak her vengeance upon the evil of the Underworld.

And, for a while, she enjoyed every bloody second of it.

Some wolves had gotten drunk off bloodlust. It didn't just happen to vampires and demons.

And they usually ended up living like rabid animals, going on a killing spree until taken down by some hunter or a larger monster.

By the time the carnage was done, Alara's fur was soaked in blood. Its hot stickiness drowned her other senses, leaving the smell of iron and life burning her nose and tongue.

They encountered no one else and burst through the exit Secret had promised. The cornfield she'd come in from lay to the right.

The sudden rush of fresh air purged her body of the bloodlust, and she started coming down off her high. Her body shook as she lost her wolf form and morphed back into a human. The dagger slipped from her grasp as her naked body fell to the ground, her breaths coming in shaky gasps. She lifted her scarlet hands, staring at the blood coating them, which was caked under her broken fingernails. She stared. And stared and stared, unable to believe what she was seeing. She was coming apart inside. "What have I done?" she whispered. "What have I done?"

In the distance, doors burst open, and guards shouted to one another, coming her way.

Get up. We have to go before they see us.

Secret forced her up, grabbing the dagger as she stumbled toward the rows of cornstalks. Her feet seemed to catch every hole and twig. She fell at least five times, palms scraping the rough earth as Secret spurred her closer to safety. It felt as if she'd had the flu, died, and then been resurrected to be hit by a bus. Her insides felt ragged, as though someone had taken a meat tenderizer to them. The overexertion of magic had left her drained, while the guilt that split her conscience wide open left her mind feeling numb.

What have I done?

You can worry about it after we save ourselves. They fell into the cornfield, and Alara spit out dirt. Her elbows shook as she lifted her body, the soil sticking to the blood that coated her skin. Like a baby, she crawled along the earth, her feet trying to find purchase only to give out again.

It was so hard to focus, so hard to think. Every cell in her body felt fried, and all she wanted to do was sleep. Close her eyes and never wake up.

Never wake up.

She smiled a little—right before a hand shot out of the corn and grabbed her.

CHAPTER FIFTEEN

Nik swore as Alara's teeth bit down onto his hand. His skin was tough but not that tough. Damn.

Pulling her to him, he said quietly into her ear, "It's me, it's me. Sssh. It's okay."

"Nik?" Her teeth let up, and she turned around to gape at him. "What are you—? How did you—?"

"Your scent, love," he said tersely, cutting her off. "Plus, I'm an Alpha, and you are part of my pack. Though you're blocking me for some reason, I can still sense our connection, dull as it is. I'll always be able to find you."

She frowned at him, and he frowned right back. "Care to explain what the hell we're doing here?"

Her eyes looked away, and he growled a sigh of exasperation. Running a hand through his hair—which he was still surprised he was able to do, considering how long it'd been since he'd last had hair this long—he said, "It's fine." It wasn't, but he wasn't about to pry at his mate. It would only cause her to clam up tighter, and he'd worked so hard this past month at getting her to trust him. He wasn't about to break that fragile trust now by being a prick.

Someone shouted from beyond the cornfield, and both their heads jerked around as they listened. "What's going on?" he said quietly, tensed for battle. "There's an alarm going off." He listened more closely. "Wait, are they looking for you?"

"We should go," she said, eyes scanning the rows of cornstalks.

He grabbed her and shook her. "What the hell, Alara? What's going on? What have you gotten yourself into? You're naked, covered in blood..." His hands began to shake.

"I had to Shift, and I can't talk about it now!" she snapped, jerking free. "We have to get out of here!"

Before he could speak, she took off at a run toward the road. Growling curses under his breath, he ran after her until they came to the road.

More footsteps and voices followed behind them, and they did not sound happy. They had to get the hell outta Dodge before whomever she'd pissed off found them.

When she started to go left, he grabbed her hand. "Hold up. I'm over here." Leading her down the road to the right, he pulled her down a gravel driveway to an old farmhouse. There sat his Porsche, gleaming silver and looking very out of place considering the surroundings.

Unlocking it with a beep, they got in and quickly buckled up. Nik punched the start/stop button and burned rubber out of the driveway, tires squealing and gravel pitching every which way as they gunned it down the highway.

"There's a change of clothes, and a towel, I think, in the backseat."

Alara immediately went for it, quickly pulling on a large navy-blue T-shirt so she didn't flash whomever they might pass. She tugged on a pair of oversized pants without attempting to get the blood off. It looked like a crap-shoot anyway. Most of it appeared dried.

The engine growled as it switched gears, and Alara laced up a pair of sneakers that looked a size or two too big. Nik made a mental note to stock more feminine clothing in the cars. They did have more female wolves in the pack now. While they weren't a high-maintenance lot, he was certain they'd appreciate clothes that fit halfway right.

He sniffed, his nose shriveling up. "Your scent is off. It's... sour. Like magic." He'd always thought magic of any color made the air smell like sunbaked milk. It hadn't been as noticeable outside, among the open sky and smells of ripe corn and freshly tilled earth. But in the confinement of the car, it was downright overpowering.

Alara didn't speak, staring out the window.

He looked at her. Her hands were gathered in her lap. And they were shaking.

He instantly softened, concern taking over. "Alara—"

"Don't," she said quietly, closing in on herself and turning farther away from him. Her hair ducked in front of her face, hiding it from view. "Please don't."

He wasn't about to give up that easily. "What were you doing in a place like that?" Gently. Nonaccusatory.

She shifted her weight, leaning farther away from him.

Okay, so this was not working. Deciding to switch tactics and wait for her to open up, he looked away, and a glimmer caught his eye. At her hip was a dagger he hadn't noticed before. He'd been too focused on all the blood coating his very naked mate.

It looked exactly like the dagger that prick king had tried to use to kill Alara...

"Where did you get that?" he started to ask but stopped. Prying clearly wasn't getting her to open up any faster. If anything, it was driving her farther away from him.

Though patience wasn't his strong suit and it killed him to do so, he turned around and faced the road. His hands flexed against the steering wheel in a weak-assed attempt to rid them of tension.

Magic stench. Ritualistic daggers. Secretive mate.

Something had to be wrong for Alara to lock down like this.

Was it him? He glanced at her sidelong. She still hadn't looked at him, still continued staring out that window as if the cows and corn were fascinating.

His heart sped up. What had he done wrong? How had he made her not trust him so soon into their bonding?

"I wish," he said quietly, "you would let me in, Alara. I wish you would let me help you. I wish you would trust me to let me help you."

"What's that supposed to mean?" she said, her voice rough. Weak.

Beyond the point of caring.

A lump formed in his throat and a knot in his stomach.

"It means since we've been back, you won't open up to me. You never have. Not truly. And I want so badly to help. Really, I do. But you won't let me."

She flinched. For a moment, it looked as if she was going to speak. Her mouth opened, she licked her lips—and then nothing. Not one damn word.

He was so fucked. God, why did he screw up every relationship he'd been in?

She's going to abandon you. Just like Elijah, Verika, Gage, your father—

Shut up! he growled at his inner voice of doubt. *Just shut the fuck up about stuff you have no idea about.*

No, he couldn't think like this, not now. Their bond was still there. Something had weakened it, yes, but it wasn't broken.

Not yet.

And he wouldn't let it. He would never willingly let Alara go. Doing so would be like ripping out his own heart. Unless she wanted to leave him. At which point, he'd let her go because he loved her so damn much, and he heard that was the thing you did when someone wanted out. If you love someone, you'll let them go, and all that shit.

That thought alone made his heart start to tear and made him go cold all over.

"I'm sorry," Alara whispered. "You're right. You're right about it all. I haven't done a very good job of letting you in. For so long at Court I was an outcast. I was taught from a very young age you couldn't trust anyone. That if you let them get too close, they'd use your weaknesses against you. They'd hurt you." A shudder rolled through her, and she hugged herself.

He started to reach for her but stopped. God, it was hard wanting to comfort his mate but being afraid to touch her for fear he'd drive her away. "I understand completely."

"I know." She finally looked at him, those gray eyes shining, and took his hand and squeezed.

He squeezed back, holding onto her hand as if it were a life raft.

A phone call on the dash broke the heavy silence. Gage's name read on the screen, replacing the name of the song that had been playing on the radio. Growling because he knew he had to take the call, he pressed a button on the steering wheel with his thumb. Bluetooth put the call through from his cell, and Gage's voice came over the car speakers.

"This a bad time?" Gage asked.

"Any time's a bad time lately," Nik said tensely. "What's up? You sound ragged."

"I haven't gotten much sleep." A yawn followed to punctuate the fact. "I've sent some contacts out into the field to gather intel on what happened with Malachite. Figured it would help you, since I know you have a lot on your plate."

Nik snorted. "You're running a nation of werewolves and trying to prevent World War Witch, and you say I have a lot on my plate?"

"Well, you've done a lot for me. I've never really been in a big enough position to do much to return the favor.

But I haven't forgotten how much you've helped me, and I'll never be able to repay you for keeping me alive in Malachite's pack."

Nik's throat grew tight. Taking a deep breath, he said gruffly, "So what's the intel? I'm guessing you found something if you called."

"You remember Marcus?"

Marcus... "Yeah, Gramps. Used to be a loner in the Moonstruck Pack. He'd been there through two Alphas and left right after Malachite took over and went homicidal." Nik had gravitated toward the man, had found a kindred spirit in him. He got the whole loner aspect, not being much of a social butterfly himself. The two rough-around-the-edges men had clicked. Right before Marcus left, he'd told Nik about sensing the growing storm and how he wanted to get out while he still could. Nik was still relatively new to the pack and very unschooled in the inner workings of pack politics. Marcus had warned him and Gage not to get involved with the Moonstruck Pack, that things were about to get real ugly, but they were desperate. No one else would take them in, not wanting two strong, capable men who'd potentially be a threat for the rank of Alpha.

Besides, they'd wanted a fresh start. And boy, had they gotten one. A slate wiped clean only to be bathed in blood.

"I had one of my guys track him down, since he seemed to know everything about everybody," Gage said. "He said he wasn't in on the killings of Malachite's family, but he gave me the names of those who possibly were."

"Does he know for sure?"

"No," Gage breathed with disappointment. "He only heard Rick say 'Gonna make him pay.' He says the pack was on hard times, and a group of them had been killing off of the property line for food, though the Alpha had warned them not to. Anyway, before long, the papers were circulating about vicious wolves running amok, killing farmers' livestock. Hunters started taking to the woods, shooting every wolf on sight. One day a pup was killed— Rick's little girl."

"Jesus." Nik ran a hand over his mouth. He knew the man wore a locket that had been hers. It had her picture in it, and every now and then he'd catch him staring at it with a sad look in his eyes. "So you think this was a revenge killing? That Malachite was the one who shot Rick's pup?"

"That's my theory."

"Thanks, man. It gives me a hell of a lot more to go off of than I had a few minutes ago."

"No problem. I'll let you know if I find out anything else useful. Still dealing with the DPI?"

"Yeah…"

"Uh-oh."

"That's an understatement," Nik muttered. His eyes flashed to a sign along the interstate for hotels and gas. "Look, man, I've gotta get off the freeway here. I'll hit you up later. Thanks again."

Gage didn't question him. The two were used to cutting conversations short, knowing when to keep it strictly business and when it was okay to linger. Today was not one of those days.

The call ended as Nik signaled, pulled off the highway,

and took a right at the stoplight.

"Where are we going?" Alara asked, looking around at the small town they were pulling into.

"We need to lie low. Those guys back at the plant sounded pissed, and I don't want to get stuck in a high-speed chase and endanger civilians."

They didn't say another word as they pulled up to a gas station nestled between a couple of old brick buildings and parked the car in the alley, out of sight of the main freeway. Across the parking lot sat a run-down farmhouse that'd been converted into a bed and breakfast. Donning sunglasses, hats, and a hoodie for Alara to cover up the blood on her arms, Nik tugged Alara into the B & B and checked for a vacancy. They were in luck—there had just been a cancellation. Or so the clerk said. It didn't appear to be busy. The place was a ghost town.

After getting the key and heading up to the second story, Nik shut the door behind them.

"Are we staying here for the night?" Alara asked.

"No. Just to hide out for a few hours. The window overlooks the main drag through this town, giving us a clear view of the parking lot. We'll know if someone fishy comes looking for us. Once nightfall has settled in, we'll head back to the manor."

"We should warn them." Alara bit her lip. "The warlock I lifted this off of"—she gestured to the dagger—"he recognized me."

"Shit." Running a hand over his face, he called his Beta and delivered the news to be on alert for intruders and to call him if said intruders invaded their property. After hanging up, he paced and at last rested his head against the warmed glass of the window. So far so good, but he knew that optimistic bullshit wouldn't last long.

Tense silence stretched between them. It felt as if the air were made out of cement, it was so thick. Nik didn't face Alara for a long time. Finally, he turned around, his face a mask of sorrowful resignation as he gazed at the mate he longed to hold but felt he couldn't touch. He didn't know her. This wasn't his Alara, this angel of death and shadows.

He silently went to the bathroom and walked out with a dampened washcloth. Kneeling before her, he proceeded to wash the blood from her face.

She watched him silently, fear and tenderness in her eyes. That glassy indifference was starting to crack. "Are you still mad at me?" she whispered.

Unable to take it anymore, he swallowed hard, dropped the rag, and took her into his arms. She instantly clung to him, digging her nails into his back. They held each other, trembling.

"I can't feel you, through our bond," he said, his deep voice ragged. "I mean, I can, but it's not the same. You're so silent. Why are you shutting me out, baby?"

"I don't mean to."

He leaned back, cupping her face in his hands. She'd started to cry. "Then why?"

Her bottom lip trembled as she searched his eyes. She looked absolutely miserable.

And scared.

He frowned. "What is it, baby? What aren't you telling me?"

She shook her head, more tears falling.

"You can tell me." He started to stroke her hair, but she smacked his hand away, rising quickly and taking a few steps away from him.

"No, I can't, Nik! I can't—oh God." She swayed, nearly going down, but he rushed to catch her. She tried pushing away, but he held firm. "All those men… I killed…"

He went still. "What men? Baby, what are you talking about?"

"I murdered them, Nik!" she whispered, lifting her red-rimmed eyes to his. "I slaughtered them because they were in my way. And… and… I enjoyed it." She squeezed her eyes shut. "I'm despicable. A horrible person."

"Were they armed?"

"Yes. They tried to stop me."

He held her tight. "They tried to kill you."

"Yes. At least, I think they would have. I don't know. I don't know, I don't know."

Her body shook with sobs, and for a brief flickering of an instant, he felt her grief open up the channel between them.

And not just grief—regret. Anger. Confusion.

All the things he'd felt the first time he'd taken a life.

"Since the dawn of time, it's been kill or be killed." He kissed the top of her head. "You did nothing wrong."

"How can you say that? I'm a horrible person."

He winced, hating the stain killing someone had left on her sweet soul.

His beautiful, innocent Alara. Forever marked by blood and death.

"I'm a killer," she said with quiet darkness. Her tears had dried, leaving her eyes red and her skin damp. Her face was blank, as if all the emotion had drained out of her.

He cupped her face and lifted it so her eyes met his. "Listen to me. You did what you had to do. There is nothing wrong with protecting yourself. Sometimes in life we have to make hard choices in unfair circumstances. Yes, those people had families. Yes, they had regular lives to get back to. But so did you. They knew that when they took the order to kill you. They were prepared to die."

"That doesn't erase the wrongness of what I've done."

"No. Nothing ever will. But you have to forgive yourself for being selfish, for fighting back. Because I can guarantee you those men, if involved with Mistress Black, which I take it they are if you have that dagger, wouldn't have given your death a second thought. You have to let it go."

They both breathed heavily in the sudden silence, digesting this. Alara cleared her throat and stepped back, hugging herself. "I need to think."

Nik's hands lingered in the air where her face had been before finally dropping to his sides. His spine went rigid, and his self-doubt flared. "Don't shut me out, Alara." He reached for her, and she stepped back, out of his grip.

It was like a slap to the face. His cheeks burned as blood rushed through them. "Have you changed your mind about our bond?" he asked, his voice cracking on the end.

"What? No."

"Is there someone else?"

"Of course not."

"Then why? Why are you keeping me at a distance?"

"I'm trying to protect you." She immediately bit down on her lip so hard she drew blood. Her eyes widened, as if even she was surprised by her actions.

"Protect me? From what?"

"She can't tell you," Alara snapped, eyes flashing silver before she whirled around.

Nik froze. He hadn't imagined that. He fucking hadn't. All this time… those people back at Crescent Manor.

And that voice. She hadn't spoken with the fear and sorrow she had earlier. This voice had been cold, sharp.

Not hers.

Watching her warily, he lifted a hand toward her shoulder. "Alara?"

Her head suddenly jerked to the window, and she crossed over to it, peering into the street below. "We have company."

Freaking A. Exactly what he needed right now. Then again, having a punching bag to vent his frustrations out on might not be such a bad idea.

Alert and focused, Nik joined his mate at the window and looked out onto the street below. Several black vehicles were pulling up to the inn, coming to a screeching halt as doors flew open and men who looked as if they'd just gotten off death row poured out. Nik sensed the warlock before he saw him, and he did not like what he felt. This guy was powerful—a Red Warlock. And he looked pissed. He was a bit thinner than the others and not quite as bulky. Plus, he had on a suit. Judging from the way the others scrambled to open his car door, he was clearly the leader of this little band of misfits. He cupped a glowing red orb in the palm of his hand, his mouth barely moving with muttered words as he followed the others inside the building.

"Tracker spell," Nik said grimly. "That's how they found us. We've gotta go."

"Jump through the window."

Nik paused, about to turn around. He looked at his mate as if she'd lost her mind. "Seriously?"

"They're coming up the stairs," she said with irritation. "That door is our only other exit, and the other rooms might be locked. Even if we make it to them, we'll be in the same predicament, stuck with either a window or a door that leads to the enemy. There aren't a lot of places to hide here. So that leaves the window."

Nik was all for a little James Bond action, but the thought of sending his mate flying out the window made him nauseous. "But what about you?"

She smiled wickedly. "What about me?"

Next thing he knew, the door behind them was being hammered on by a pair of fists or maybe a boot.

Alara backed up and ran for the window. There was the sound of shattering glass, and she was gone.

Eyes wide at what his ladylike princess had just done, he glanced at the door. The lock was starting to crack the doorframe. It wouldn't hold much longer.

"Fuck me," he muttered then bolted for the window as the door flew off its hinges.

Gunfire blasted the wall around him as he zigzagged

and leapt through the window.

His fall was broken by the roof overlooking the porch. He slid down it and landed on his feet in a crouch on the ground.

"Come on!" Alara yelled from their car, which she'd pulled up to the curb.

He frowned. How in the hell had she gotten it so fast?

The stench of magic stung his nose as he got in, and she sped off.

"What the hell's going on?" he demanded. "I think I have a right to know, considering I was just shot at."

She smiled faintly. "That's exactly what I said."

"What? What are you talking about?"

The growl of engines fell in line behind them as several black vehicles appeared in the rearview mirror.

"Shit," Alara muttered, switching gears. The car surged forward as she fed it more gas, and she wove around cars. Here, the highway only had two lanes. He gripped the leather seat as she passed another car, missing a honking semi by mere feet.

He looked at this woman beside him, this alien creature.

Where had Alara gone?

Where was the woman who chastised him for swearing too much at formal events? Who teased him if his bowtie was crooked? Where was the lover who tenderly whispered his name as she raked her manicured nails down his back?

Where was his mate?

Something popped, and the back end of the car spun.

Gritting his teeth, he held on to the "oh shit!" handle as Alara fought for control of the car. Pieces of tire flew away from the rear passenger side of the Porsche, and he saw a man with a gun smile at them from the vehicle directly behind them. While admiring that it was a damn good shot, Nik couldn't help but sense that they were royally fucked.

"*Shit!*"

He looked up—right in time to see an SUV ram into them.

The impact rattled his bones. The screech of metal, the sensation of the car pitching into the ditch and flipping. The world spun in a mixture of green and blue as the sky and ground tumbled around one another before the car at last came to a stop, upside down.

His vision blurred as he blinked rapidly. It felt as if someone were squeezing his head like a piece of fruit, threatening to squash it at any time.

Sounds cut in and out of clarity. Behind them, back toward the highway, several cars screeched to a halt. Doors opened, and footsteps thundered toward them.

He glanced over at Alara. Blood dripped down her chin from some wound he couldn't see. Her eyes were closed.

Heart instantly in his throat, he rasped, "Alara?"

She didn't respond.

Darkness pulled at him, lining his vision with pitch black, but he refused to go under. Not yet. Not before he saw to his mate's safety.

Reaching out with their bond, he heaved a sigh of relief when he felt her life force. Unconscious but not severely wounded. And definitely not dead.

Though the guys gathering outside their wrecked car might be about to change their luck.

Struggling with the seat belt that was apparently stuck in its buckle, he gritted his teeth as he saw them lift their guns to his vehicle.

No. No, not like this. Their lives were supposed to end on a porch of a little farmhouse, somewhere far in the country of some backwoods town no one had ever heard of. Where the politics of the Underworld couldn't get to them, and they could live out the remainder of their lives in peace while sipping sweet tea or lemonade or whatever the fuck it was old people drank.

"No," he growled, still jiggling the seatbelt. "Give, damn you!"

From the road, Nik heard the wail of police sirens.

"DPI!" someone shouted, and the crowd dispersed like a herd of antelope that had just spotted a leopard.

Tires shrieked as they drove off, and the sirens drew closer.

Alara, was all he thought before giving in to the lingering darkness, unable to hold out any longer.

The sensation of being safe wrapped around him.

Which was really stupid, wishful thinking. If there was one thing he'd learned, it was that they were never truly safe.

Not until Mistress Black was dead.

CHAPTER SIXTEEN

VERYTHING WAS DARK, AND THEN IT WASN'T. PATCHES of color burst through the darkness, cutting away at the shadows until she was standing in a forest. A huge white oak stood in front of her, as wide as it was tall, its large branches contrasting against the gold and red leaves. The entire forest was a kaleidoscope of crimson, green, orange, brown, and yellow. The chill of deep autumn hung in the air, and she hugged herself. Sunshine polka-dotted the forest floor, warming the air slightly. Dust motes danced in the beams of sunshine, looking like glitter.

High above the ground, nestled at the head of the white oak's trunk, was a large tree house.

Alara smiled.

Making her way over to it, she carefully climbed the ladder that had been nailed to the tree. The boards had been worn smooth in places, having been climbed by Izzy and Alara many times while they were growing up. It was a haven, a safe house. A place to get away from Court politics, from Mother and Father and the life she resented at times because it made her feel trapped.

Alara didn't spook when she climbed into the tree house and found her sister waiting there. Somehow, she already knew Izzy was there.

Old velvet pillows with golden tassels and bookcases full of fairy tales decorated the small room, which was only large enough to hold maybe four adults but had seemed like a palace when they were younger and smaller.

Mimicking her sister's posture and sitting cross-legged, she looked out the little curtained window into the forest.

The silence grew thick, uncomfortable. Alara hadn't noticed at first how still Izzy had gotten, but the fact that her sister had yet to look at or speak to her hadn't gone unnoticed.

"You disappointed me," Izzy finally said quietly. Still not looking at her.

Those words felt like a hammer's blow to Alara's heart. "I tried my best."

"You didn't fight."

"I did."

"No, you didn't!"

Alara blinked at the savagery in Izzy's ladylike voice. There was something off about it, a snarl, a growl, a gurgle.

Alara's brows furrowed. "You weren't there. You're not here. You don't know what it's like, living day after day without you. Knowing I can never bring you guys back, that I've failed you."

"No, sister. You failed me the moment you became a murderer."

Alara's neck prickled with icicles.

"I felt it, your enjoyment and satisfaction as you took their lives. Have felt your guilt whenever you remember Father telling you Mother had been killed and you sigh inwardly in relief. You're evil, after all."

"No." Alara shook her head then cleared her throat so she could speak louder. "No, you don't understand. They were going to kill me."

"Maybe you should have let them. Done the world a favor."

"Izzy," Alara breathed, reeling from the blow. "This isn't you."

Izzy's shoulders shook as she coughed violently. She covered her mouth with her hand, and the metallic tang of fresh blood filled the air. Crimson coated the inside of Izzy's hand when she pulled it back. Izzy slowly looked at her sister, face pale as death, a dribble of blood spilling out of her mouth. Her eyes were black pits, threatening to suck Alara's soul into them. "You're evil, Alara. Look what you did to me. Because the Order couldn't kill you, they killed me instead."

Alara scrambled away, standing. "No. No, I didn't do this. It's not my fault!"

"It is your fault!" Izzy bellowed in the voice of a demon, also standing. The sunlight outside dried up, chased away by gathering storm clouds. An icy gale ripped through the trees, making the leaves rattle. Izzy pointed to the window. "Look at what you've done! Sent all of us to early graves!"

Alara didn't want to, but she did—she looked.

There, on the ground far below, the earth was stirring. Hands shot out of the damp soil, clawing at the earth as the bodies pulled themselves free.

Alara stopped breathing.

One by one, the corpses stood, covered in dirt and blood.

Blood that she had spilled.

There they were, the men she'd killed back at the plant. And Mother, a large red wound in her chest. On the end was Father, his fine clothes torn to shreds by her claw marks, his neck bent at an odd angle and his throat ripped out. Where the corpses' eyes should have been sat two empty, black sockets.

"I had a pup and a mate waiting for me at home," one of the guards said.

"My sick mother will die without me!" another wailed.

"You should have let me kill you," said her father.

Tears ran down Alara's face as she walked to the window. "I'm sorry. I'm so, so sorry."

"Not sorry enough," Izzy said, now directly behind her. "Not yet."

Izzy shoved her, and Alara toppled over the window's edge, screaming as she plummeted toward the hissing corpses, their bony hands stretched wide to grab her.

She gasped for air, eyes snapping open as she shot up off the gurney. The paramedic immediately went for her. "Calm down, miss. You took quite the blow. Please, lie back down."

Alara's scrambled brain quickly took in her

surroundings. No darkening forest, no roiling, ominous storm clouds, no vengeful corpses waiting to tear her apart. Just the inside of an ambulance. Which should have worried her, but considering her nightmare, it seemed like a very safe, ordinary place in comparison.

With a long sigh, she lay back down and closed her eyes. God, she was exhausted. And her body hurt all over.

The paramedic checked her vitals again. "Do you remember your name?"

"Alara. Alara Crescent."

"Do you remember what happened, Alara?"

Not at first, she didn't. The sound of bending metal, the screech of tires, the sensation of spinning, of falling, all came back to her in a blur. She opened her mouth to speak, but Secret stopped her. Opening her eyes, she said, "Yes. But you won't."

Alara seized the paramedic's head, eyes flashing silver as the bewitchment began. "There's been a change of plans. We're not going to a hospital. You're going to take me home."

You'd think as many times as Nik had been knocked out, he'd be used to the pain of waking up. The ringing in the ears, the headache, the general "what the fuck?" of it all.

His head bumped against something cushy, not quite as soft as a pillow, and it crinkled when he moved his head, like plastic. The sound of an engine and tires rolling over road were the next things he picked up on. He was in some kind of vehicle, going someplace he probably didn't want to go.

Now, when you first came to and you didn't know where the fuck you were, you didn't open your eyes right away and alert your captor that you were awake. Doing a limb check—dumb as it sounded—he tried discreetly moving his wrists and ankles. They moved all right, but not by much. Something cold and metallic clanked against something else metallic. He didn't even have to look to know what that sound meant. Someone had handcuffed him to something. Something, something, something…

Stifling a groan, he cracked his eyes open a sliver and squinted against the bright white light shining down on him. Suddenly, someone pulled his eyelids wide open, and he hissed. Fuck, it was as if he were two feet away from the sun, it was so bright. Growling, he jerked his head away.

"Oh, sorry!" said a female voice. The light immediately vanished. "I didn't realize you were awake."

When the spots before his eyes cleared, Nik saw an older woman—a Blue Witch—standing there, clad in the uniform of the Underworld's paramedics. He'd always thought the uniforms were boring as hell, but whatever. He didn't have to wear one.

Navy-blue button-down tucked into navy-blue pants, with a black belt and black shoes. The letters DPI and a Rod of Asclepius were embroidered in gold thread on the left breast pocket.

As he said, very trendy.

He looked around now. Duh. He was in an ambulance. The squishy, plastic-like thing he was lying on was a stretcher. And because he was so polite, the first thing that popped out of his mouth was, "Where the fuck is my mate, and who the fuck are you?"

"I'm fucking Paramedic Amber Dawson," the woman said with a wry smile. "And your mate is in the ambulance ahead of us. You can't sense her? Then again, maybe your senses haven't fully recovered yet. You both took quite a blow." She grimaced.

That was an understatement. If by "took quite a blow" she meant "you were hit upside the head with a two-by-four," then maybe they were on the same page.

Nik immediately nibbled his lip. The bond between him and Alara was still muted.

Damn.

"Don't worry," Amber said. "The other paramedics just radioed me and told me your mate was fine."

"You'll pardon me if I don't believe you until I see her."

"I wouldn't expect you to be much of an Alpha, or a mate, if you didn't," she replied steadily.

He observed this woman with newfound respect. For a crummy DPI agent, she was all right.

"So it goes without saying we're heading for a trip to the police station?" Nik said.

"Maybe after we evaluate you at the hospital." Amber didn't look up from scribbling on a chart.

Damn. The two last places he wanted to be, because they were both gigantic time sucks. His pack needed him. He knew his Beta could handle things, but still... These fuckers would keep him in a cell forever just to spite him. Or a doctor would want to do X-rays and keep him overnight "just for observation."

"Hey, I'm feeling fine," he said. "I've been through worse, believe it or not."

"Not surprising. You are a wolf. We're still taking *both* of you to the hospital."

Hell, he knew he was screwed even before opening his mouth. If Alara was going to the hospital, he definitely wasn't leaving her side. This time, he was choosing her over the pack.

"Besides, we're almost there." Amber glanced at her watch and frowned. "At least, it shouldn't be too much longer."

"What's wrong?" Nik asked, studying her face.

She shook her head. "Nothing. Watch must be running out of juice."

Nik brushed it off. His mind was too preoccupied with worry for his mate. That silver gleam in her eyes, the vicious edge to her voice, those stunt-driver antics behind the wheel… it wasn't her. Nothing about that dark creature had been even remotely similar to the Alara he knew.

She was good, down to her core, and cautious. Perhaps overly so at times.

So what the fuck was wrong? Why was she acting this way? Had she reached a breaking point with her grief and just snapped?

The ambulance slowed, the sound of gravel crunching under the tires now. Amber's frown deepened as she looked out the back window. "The hell?" she muttered. She tapped on the window to the cab. "Hey! Where are we? What's going on?"

The ambulance stopped, and the driver got out

without responding. The back doors to the ambulance opened. Another paramedic, a man Nik didn't recognize, stood there, his expression blank.

"Hey, Johnnie, what the hell?" Amber said. "What are you doing? We have orders to—"

"Orders have changed," Johnnie said in a monotone voice, eyes flashing silver. Lifting a gun, he fired.

Amber's body jerked. Blood leaked out of the wound in her chest. Staring down in horror and gaping at her partner, she fell to the floor of the ambulance.

Nik jerked at his cuffs as Johnnie and another paramedic dragged the now-dead Amber out of the ambulance before grabbing his stretcher and wheeling him outside.

"What the hell is wrong with you?" Nik growled. "Who the hell are you, really?"

He stopped and stared. The manor. They were back at Crescent Manor. But why would they bring him here?

"Because I told them to, darling."

A chill went through Nik. Craning his neck, he looked over his shoulder.

Surrounding him was a crowd composed of his wolves and the DPI agents who'd been hanging out at the manor.

And standing at their center was his mate, her beautiful eyes shining brightest silver.

CHAPTER SEVENTEEN

Nik didn't take his eyes off Alara. He didn't even fucking blink. "Alara?" he asked quietly.

"For the most part," came her response, in that same monotone voice that'd come out of the mouth of the murderous paramedic.

And, come to think of it, out of the mouth of that girl they'd thrown in the dungeon. The one who'd been possessed by the doppelgänger.

He thought back to the corpse they'd found in the woods. She'd spelled out E-Y-E-S in the dirt.

That silvery glint he'd been seeing…

E-Y-E-S.

It had been a warning.

"Son of a bitch!" he roared, thrashing on the stretcher. The metal railings groaned, and the whole thing threatened to tip over. Glaring at those damnable silver eyes, he growled, "Get the hell out of my mate!"

Alara didn't move, still smiling down at him as if she were privy to some secret he wasn't. "In due time, young pup. I have use for her first."

The thought of that thing living inside of her, controlling her and making her do God knew what... Nik would rather rip his own heart out before subjecting Alara to that.

Suddenly, her strange behavior made sense. The food processing plant, the dagger, the fleeting glimpses of terror in her eyes...

Damn it! Why did he have to be such a blockhead? Why the hell hadn't he seen this sooner?

Because you've been preoccupied with the DPI and trying to keep your pack from revolting.

He stopped. "Wait a second..." he breathed, gears turning in his head. He looked around at the crowd, at the shifting, silvery sheen in the many lifeless eyes staring back at him. "You're inside all their heads. You used them to distract me, to keep me from looking too closely at Alara so you could do with her as you wanted."

"You're only partially correct," the doppelgänger said, strolling over to his side. "I did use them as a distraction, yes. Close as you werewolves tend to be to your mates, I knew you'd be a problem. But I can't be inside more than one head at once—that's impossible for my kind. I did, however, use the hypnotic powers of a very special witch."

"The corpse we found in the woods," he said flatly.

"Yes."

"What about the paramedics?"

"I stole that witch's power and used it on them too."

No remorse, not even a blink. His Alara would have been mortified. God, it was so hard to look at her, those silver eyes a reminder that he had failed to protect her.

She's still in there. I know she is. And I swear, if it costs me my life, I'm going to free her.

"You've been planning this for a while," Nik said.

"Of course. I knew once I got inside your pack and you realized what I was, you'd call the DPI first. I infiltrated them weeks ago. Then I silently made my rounds in your woods, courtesy of a shadow and cloaking spell, and hypnotized your perimeter guards."

Thus why they hadn't reported any disturbances to him. Fuck.

"All it took was a single word to activate the hypnosis. Imagine my delight when Penelope turned out to be decent enough at that trick that I could hypnotize the rest of your pack."

"You were inside Penelope too?" He paused. "The backfired spell… you got inside her then."

"Opening up a tunnel of magic to someone's mind is one of the easiest ways for my kind to infiltrate another host. Luckily for us we're so rare that the lore surrounding us is sketchy at best."

He glanced at the dagger. The doppelgänger had strapped it to Alara's hip. "What's your endgame? Why us, and why go to all this trouble?"

"You'll see soon enough. You're not the only one trying to save the world."

"Except you've hurt a hell of a lot more people."

"In every war, there are sacrifices," it said coldly. "It

doesn't make the cause any less noble." It glanced at its watch—or rather, Alara's watch—and snapped its fingers. "Take him to the dungeon."

Nik growled low as it stroked his face, like petting a favorite dog. "It'll all be over soon. And then this world will finally be safe."

The touch of Alara's skin, so cold and clammy, haunted him as they carted him away on the stretcher toward the manor.

Alara screamed inwardly as she watched her mate being taken away to rot in the dungeon of his own home. Her soul punched, kicked, and bit, howling like a wild animal, and still the doppelgänger's hold on her hadn't eased.

You'll only waste your strength, Secret said. *You need to recuperate—otherwise you might not be strong enough to take back possession of your body once I release you.*

Wasn't that your plan all along? she said bitterly. *To ensure I'm beaten down enough that I can't possibly resist you?*

Perhaps.

Chills went through Alara. This thing was evil, pure and simple.

Why hadn't she gone with her gut? Why hadn't she fought harder? Had she missed opportunities? Had she just not tried hard enough?

Because you were weak, Izzy's voice whispered. *You wanted someone else to take over, and they did. Now look at where you are.*

It was time for Alara to stop ghosting through her life

and start living it. She couldn't continue to live in the past. Doing so was literally destroying her future.

She had to save herself. And not just for her own well-being but also her pack's and her mate's.

But how?

Despair threatened to crush her. *No,* she told herself firmly. *You will not give in. You are strong, far stronger than you give yourself credit for.*

And she was. Hadn't that strength helped her survive the trials and backstabbing at Court? Hadn't it helped her get out of bed every morning after she'd left Crescent Castle for good, even though all she'd wanted to do was sleep forever?

No, she was strong. Strong enough to weather the courtiers' ridicule, strong enough to keep breathing after she'd lost her family, strong enough to keep on living.

She was ready, finally. Ready to fight for her own damn life.

The wolf joined her, growling, silently waiting for its prey to slip up…

Secret snapped her fingers at Ralph, too busy coordinating its troops to pay much attention to Alara's inner monologue. The gruff man strutted over to them, eyes glowing with an eerie silvery light. "Go with them to the dungeon. Make sure our pup behaves himself."

"Yes, ma'am," Ralph said, without any inflection, and strode toward the manor.

Secret then ordered the DPI to set up a perimeter along with the normal perimeter guards and to let her know if anyone crossed over into its land.

Its land. Not Alara's, not Nik's, not the pack's.

This damn thing was planning on putting down roots.

Not if I can stop it, Alara thought darkly. Her energy might be weak, but her anger was strong. It could fuel her, as it had those long weeks following her family's murders.

"I'm going to rest," Secret announced. "Do not disturb me unless it's an emergency."

The crowd bowed and dispersed, and Secret strolled toward the manor, its gait easy.

What are you up to? Alara demanded.

You'll see—

Don't feed me that bullshit line! I'm done entertaining your cryptic messages. You'll give me straight answers from now on.

Or you'll what?

Alara slammed on the brakes, and her body came to an abrupt halt.

Secret startled and then laughed. *I see you still have a few tricks up your sleeve.*

Alara silently fumed, waiting.

Secret cocked a brow. *May I continue, Your Highness?*

There was no mockery to the title. If anything, it sounded as though Secret respected Alara more for what she'd just done.

And Alara had learned something. Secret was becoming more comfortable in her body. Which meant she was getting careless.

Good.

Alara gave Secret back control, lurking just below the surface of her body's consciousness, ready to fight if need be.

I'm—we're—*performing a ceremony,* Secret said, continuing their walk.

The word "ceremony" sent ice-cold dread through her. She thought of an altar, a room filled with candles and magic, and her father standing over her, holding a dagger over her heart.

It was suddenly difficult to swallow. *What kind of ceremony?*

The kind where we break the spell that's been slowly resurrecting Mistress Black, Secret said, tapping the dagger. *These daggers were given to high-ranking members of the Order. They're enchanted so any life they take ships the soul straight to Mistress Black.*

What does she use the souls for?

To piece together her own soul, which was fractured hundreds of years ago when Mistress Black was captured, killed, and cursed so her body could never be resurrected for her to unleash her vengeance upon the world. Somehow she found a way around that.

So my family's souls are a part of Mistress Black now? Alara asked, mortified.

Afraid so.

How do I release them?

By killing Mistress Black. That, by the way, I can assist with, if you'll let me stay in your body once the ceremony is done.

She's baiting you, trying to trick you, Alara thought to herself. *No, thanks,* Alara thought aloud to Secret. *I'll take my chances.*

Suit yourself. As you can see, I can be a valuable ally in battle.

It could. The doppelgänger's knowledge of fighting techniques and magical prowess were vast. That kind of firepower would come in handy against one of the most powerful witches the Underworld had ever seen.

But at what cost? Did she honestly expect Secret to use her body "for the greater good" and immediately vacate after they'd won?

No way in hell.

She entered the manor and immediately went upstairs to the master suite Nik and Alara shared. The same two guards as before stood sentinel. "I'm not to be disturbed unless it's an emergency," Secret said to them.

They nodded, and Secret entered the suite, shutting and locking the door.

The room was the same as they'd left it. Alara wondered if, when this was all over, she'd ever be able to sleep soundly in here again. This was where she was taken over, where her free will was chained…

Where her life became the stuff of nightmares.

A shudder rolled through her.

I always keep my word, you know, Secret said quietly. *The Fey cannot break promises. Once we have performed the final rite, I will vacate your body.*

The ceremony you were talking about while we were walking here.

Yes, exactly. Secret took off Alara's shoes and stretched her legs. Alara's whole body felt as if she'd just run a marathon without any prep work. Every muscle was sore, and whenever she took a step, needle-like pain shot through the sole of her right foot, and her knee popped. Yes, she'd definitely "fucked some things up," as Nik would put it.

Nik.

What are you planning on doing with my mate?

Just keeping him in a safe place, for now.

Alara caught the hidden warning. If she didn't behave, the doppelgänger would use him as leverage.

Damn Secret.

So you honestly believe the ceremony, this final rite, will stop Mistress Black once and for all? Alara asked.

Yes. The ceremony will break the spell that sends souls to repair hers, preventing her from being resurrected.

But won't she just be able to cast another spell to finish the job?

Not with what we're about to do. This should also re-lease all those souls so they may find peace, rendering her powerless.

Alara raised a brow, surprised the ancient Fey would care anything for others' spiritual well-being.

Secret glanced at the clock hanging on the wall. *It'll be dark in a few hours. At dusk, we perform the rite. We'll need to rest this body before then if we're to have enough energy to fuel my magic.* They went to the bathroom to shower. Alara hesitated to strip, suddenly very shy, despite the fact that she'd been naked earlier after Shifting. *I'll let you wash in private. Don't worry,* Secret said.

Alara stared at the steamy water longingly.

Don't you want to get the grime and blood off? Secret said.

Blood. Somehow her mind had pushed the image of all those dead guards out of her head, a self-defense mechanism perhaps to keep her from unraveling. But the word "blood" sent those images hurtling forward in her mind's eye, tearing through her conscience and making her guilt feel like iron chains wrapped around her heart.

Alara's lip trembled as Secret undressed them and climbed into the shower. As the hot water hit her face and steam perforated the air, Alara felt Secret's presence fade, and she began to sob.

For the family she couldn't protect.

For the men whose lives she'd taken in cold blood.

And, most of all, for the last bit of innocence in her that had died when she'd done it.

CHAPTER EIGHTEEN

THE THING ABOUT BEING LOCKED AWAY IN A DUNGEON meant you had a lot of free time on your hands. Nik welcomed it, because he had a lot to think about.

He'd been pacing relentlessly since they'd locked him up in here a few hours ago, mulling over everything again and again until he thought he'd go insane.

How could he have missed it? He'd sensed something was wrong with his mate, but he'd been too distracted by all this other bullshit to pay attention to it.

Because the doppelgänger wanted you to be distracted, his logic said. *You did nothing wrong.*

Which was bullshit—he'd failed her. Not only that, but he'd failed this pack when he'd let that thing take over.

He pounded a fist against the wall, rattling the bars. How could he have been so stupid and so blind?

Not much was known about doppelgängers. They usually weren't this careless or this reckless.

Which made him wonder... was this thing on a suicide mission? Had it finally gotten to a point where its supposedly "noble cause" was worth more than keeping the secrets of its species?

That thought scared him the most.

It said, after all, that it had been trying to save the world. Did it mean by stopping Mistress Black? Was that why it had Alara go after that dagger? Whose side was this fucking thing on?

Guilt wracked him. He'd never felt more like a failure in his life. He'd felt guilty when Mom, Dad, and Elijah had left, as if it were somehow his fault. Which was stupid. He knew they'd made their own decisions, and he'd made peace with that long ago.

But this... maybe it was his fault.

He leaned his head against the cool metal bars, breathing deeply and closing his eyes.

So what if it was? The one good thing his dad had taught him was to own up to his mistakes. He would make this right. He had to. He had people counting on him. His mate needed him, now more than ever.

Hold on, Alara. I promise I'll set you free.

He didn't know how, he didn't know when. But when he made a promise, he damn well kept it.

Voices approaching jerked his attention upward, toward the stairs. His hackles rose, and his inner wolf growled as Ralph appeared along with three other men from the perimeter watch. Counting the two guards already on duty, that made five.

Nik grinned. He was almost insulted if this was all the

doppelgänger had sent after him.

"Time to go, hotshot," Ralph said, smirking as he unlocked the door to Nik's cell. "My boss has big plans for you."

"Funny. I thought I was your boss." Two men stepped forward to grab Nik by the arms to lead him out.

"Not anymore." Ralph glared at him. "I can't say I won't enjoy this."

"Nor can I say the same for this."

Summoning his strength, Nik jerked free and quickly dispatched the two guards who'd been holding him. "Not cuffing me was your first mistake."

The remaining two guards, standing alongside Ralph, raised their guns. "Wait!" Ralph brought up a hand. "She needs him alive."

"What for?" Nik demanded.

"Don't know. Wouldn't tell us. But I'm sure it's nothing you don't deserve, you piece of filth."

"Why do you hate me so much?" Nik couldn't care less, but he kept talking, hoping to distract Ralph long enough to form an escape plan.

"Because you think you're tough. You think you know loss." Ralph's voice warbled a little. "But you don't. You don't know shit."

Nik stared at him. The hurt, longing, and regret shining in the other wolf's eyes twisted at his heart.

And in that moment, he knew he couldn't hurt him.

"Sorry, fellas," Nik said. "I'm afraid I can't participate in whatever flawed plan this doppelgänger has thought of." Quick as a shadow, he lunged for the guard to Ralph's right, the smallest of the three, and disarmed him before he could draw breath. Nik hooked an arm around the guy's throat, holding him to his chest as he pointed the gun at his head.

Was he going to pull the trigger? Hell no. But they didn't know that.

And if there was one thing he was damn good at, it was playing poker.

Ralph and the other guy—Nate, Nik finally remembered—growled at him. Their eyes flashed gold, warring with the silver. "That's low for an Alpha," Ralph said. "But I suppose we shouldn't be surprised."

"Never underestimate a Johnson," Nik said, grinning like a kid up to no good. Shoving the hostage at them, he fired a round into the overhead fluorescent lighting. The bulbs shattered, sending a shower of sparks and glass raining down on the three wolves. They ducked, throwing up their hands to partially shield them.

Nik bolted.

Bounding up the stairs, he burst through the door and down the hall, heading for the main storage room. Since it was filled with magical paraphernalia, there had to be something in there that he could use to stop the doppelgänger. He needed to help Alara, even if he died trying. On one hand, he could try to leave and run for help. But he didn't want to leave his mate vulnerable to the whims of that monster, and besides, he didn't know if she'd even be here when he got back. Or what the doppelgänger would have her do while he was gone. He couldn't risk everyone else's safety any more than he could risk hers.

For all he knew, that thing could take Alara and every-one he cared about straight to Mistress Black. It had said it'd been running from her, but that could just as easily have been a lie. But if it actually was running away, why? What had it done? Was it an escaped prisoner and wanted revenge for what Mistress Black had done to it? Or maybe it was lying. Was it really part of Mistress Black's extend-ed network of spies, sent to destroy them from the inside out? Was the whole "running in fear" thing a sob story meant to trick them into letting their guards down so it could kill them all more easily? His heart threatened to cave in on itself in a black hole of heartache. The thought of losing Alara forever was unbearable.

The storage room wasn't far, thankfully, since it was located on the lower levels of the manor. Running for it, he quickly shut the door, knowing someone had to have seen him come down this way. Suddenly the extra secu-rity cameras he'd had installed in a moment of paranoia, believing he was keeping his pack safe, sounded like a fucking stupid idea.

C'est la vie.

Looking around quickly, he scanned row after row of bottled potions and dusty spellbooks. This room had nev-er sat well with him. The air stank of magic, which clung to the worn pages of the spellbooks like cheap cologne.

He stopped before a glowing, golden bottle. It looked… hopeful.

Unfortunately, the label was in some language he couldn't read.

Damn. Too bad there wasn't a Hooked on Phonics for paranormal languages.

"I wouldn't try that if I were you."

He whirled around.

CHAPTER NINETEEN

NIK FROZE. "PEN?"

The witch stepped forward, her eyes flickering with silvery light.

He growled in frustration. Damn, had the doppelgänger gotten to everyone?

As he did in any potential fighting situation, he pushed his weight to the balls of his feet, prepared to flee.

Or fight. But he really didn't want to fuck with Penelope. For one, she was a friend. For two, she could flick her wrist and fuck him up six ways from Sunday.

He was so not in the mood for that right now.

"How did you—" he started.

"Know you were here?" she finished. She pointed to the doorway. Nik hadn't noticed it before, but the frame glowed faintly with silvery light. "You tripped my alarm. I set it before I left to convene with the Council."

"And I'll bet that creepy-ass monster had you tell them

everything's fine, right?"

"Yep. Everything is fine and dandy, as they say. Nothing to see here." She smiled tightly. "Shall we begin?"

"Ladies first." He ducked as she shot out a hand and sent a net of pure-white light hurtling toward him. As he'd done so many times, he tucked his head in and rolled along the floor, coming up onto his feet and taking off at a dead run through the storeroom.

"You can't hide from me, Nik," Penelope called lazily. "Come out. Together, we can stop Mistress Black. Isn't that what you wanted?"

"Not like this," he muttered to himself, hiding behind a large metal bookcase full of spellbooks.

Fuck. This wasn't going according to plan. Looking at the rows of stocked shelving in front of him, he frantically scanned them for anything remotely useful. Shit. Why hadn't he taken potions more seriously, really taken the time to come down here and learn what the hell all this stuff did? Some of it he couldn't even pronounce.

"Marco?" Penelope called. When her voice was met with silence, she laughed. "Can't blame me for trying."

Her footsteps were getting closer.

"Fuck," he swore quietly. Grabbing a bunch of shit and praying it was useful, he shoved the little bottles in his pockets and peered around the corner of the bookcase. Penelope came into view, idly looking around, as if she were shopping and not trying to capture him or kill him or whatever she'd been charged to do.

His heart pounded as he braced himself, waiting. Once she'd stepped in front of the bookcase, he said,

"Sorry, Penelope," and shoved hard.

The bookcase creaked and fell, right on top of a shrieking Penelope.

Nik didn't wait around to see if she was all right. He knew she would be. Pen had started off her magical career by serving in the DPI for twenty years, after all.

Taking off at a run, he bolted around the toppled bookcase and mess of broken bottles and books and ran for the exit.

Something whooshed through the air, lassoing around his foot and yanking him forward. He fell, knocking the wind from his chest and banging his skull against the cold concrete floor. His body slid across the floor, away from the exit and toward a very pissed-off witch.

Nik didn't think he'd ever seen Penelope with a hair out of place on her head. Her hair was in disarray, and her blue dress was stained with an assortment of colored liquids. Cuts marred her skin, which were rapidly healing thanks to the regenerative powers of White Magic. "That was a low blow, Nik," she seethed, pulling on the lasso she'd created from white light. "I was going to take it easy on you, but now you've just pissed me off."

As he fought to make his lungs work, he struggled for the knife he always kept tucked in his pocket. There. Flipping the switchblade out, he cut at the lasso, only to feel as if he'd stuck his hand in a light socket. "Fuck!" His palm glared bright red, and he was about to fling the knife with another curse when he thought better of it. It still might come in handy. Tucking it back into his pocket, he grabbed one of the bottles randomly and uncorked it.

"Here goes."

He threw it at Penelope.

A boom shook the room, rattling the potions on the shelves and making his teeth sing. Penelope screamed as thousands of tiny spiders crawled from every nook and cranny of the room, covering her with their spindly legs and tiny bodies.

Penelope was terrified of spiders. Perfect.

The lasso of light vanished as she shrieked and clawed at them. Feeling sorry for her but knowing he'd be a fool if he stayed, Nik staggered to his feet and stumbled toward the exit.

He lumbered through the halls, steadying himself on the wall whenever he got dizzy. The back of his head hurt.

Not really knowing where he was going, he blindly ran, trusting his body's instincts. A remote hallway in the far corner of the manor came into view, where he knew a secret exit lay hidden behind a tapestry.

If he could just get to it—

"Going somewhere?"

"Fuck me," he growled, stopping and turning around to glare at Ralph.

The woodsman stood there with his shotgun in both hands, a mean glint in his silver eyes. "Prick." Ralph pumped the barrel. "I've put up with your shit because you're my Alpha, but not anymore."

"So you're, what? Gonna shoot me? That's taking the easy way out, isn't it?" When Ralph stilled, Nik went on. "Oh, what's the matter, Ralphie? Afraid to fight me by yourself? Terrified I'll kick your ass?"

Ralph spat and set the shotgun down on the floor. "Bullshit. You might've caught me off guard back in the dungeon, but that won't happen again." He stalked forward, and the fight was on.

Ralph led with a punch Nik saw coming from the next county. "Poor form," Nik said, blocking him easily and giving him a love tap on the jaw. "You'll never land a punch, not throwing those haymakers."

"Shut up!" Ralph swung again, too slow, and Nik deflected his punch and elbowed Ralph squarely between the ribs. The other wolf's eyes watered, and he swore. "You opened yourself up to that one. Always block your insides," Nik said, standing with his hands at his sides.

"Ah!" Ralph's face red with rage, he came swinging at Nik like a wild man. Nik snorted, slapping away the punches and kicking out toward Ralph's gut.

To his shock, Ralph just grunted and dove for him, taking them both to the floor. The man had about fifty pounds worth of gut protecting his belly, which Nik definitely felt now. The man outweighed him by at least that much, maybe more. Nik's feet struggled to find purchase, to buck Ralph off or at least get a good punch to the face in so he could distract him enough to get away.

Fuck. He shouldn't have gotten cocky. Stupid arrogance, always getting him into trouble.

The two men grappled for dominance, Nik squirming like a worm while Ralph chuckled. "Doesn't feel so good not being the big dog on top, does it?" He pressed his elbow into Nik's windpipe, and Nik choked.

Shifting his nails into claws, he stabbed at Ralph's

meaty arm, shredding his flesh. Ralph didn't seem to feel a thing.

Son of a bitch.

Nik started to see stars.

Alara's face burst through his mind, giving him renewed strength. He had a mate to save.

Gathering his power, he head-butted Ralph. The wolf yowled, his hold loosening enough for Nik to buck him off and roll to the side. He bumped into the gun, and he grabbed it as he rose to his feet.

He aimed the barrel of the gun at Ralph, who slowly rose.

Blood ran down his lip from his nose, which was set at a crooked angle. He spat onto the floor near Nik's feet. "Go ahead," Ralph rasped. "Pull the trigger."

Nik kept his index finger pressed against the trigger, ready to fire should the need arise. "Revenge."

"What?"

"That was the reason you killed Malachite's family. He killed your pup, so you killed his." He needed to know the truth, needed to hear it from the mouth of the accused party.

Ralph's eyes flashed with pain. He still mourned the passing of his daughter after all these years. Nik couldn't blame him. He'd be eaten up with grief inside if his only pup were brutally murdered like an animal.

"You may think I'm a monster, but he deserved it," Ralph said, bitterness making his words brittle.

"He was a farmer. And a hunter. He had to have been provoked," Nik said, playing off of what Gage had given him earlier.

"We didn't provoke him."

"You trespassed on his land. Killed his livestock. Made him think he had a wolf problem, which he set out to resolve."

"We were starving! We didn't have a choice! That fool Alpha Byron pissed off a Green Warlock, who bewitched the game on our land. Drove them off. Damaged all our crops too, and the edible shit in the forest."

So it really was just one big tragic misunderstanding. Nik's shoulders slumped. What a waste. Another senseless, bloody battle that could've been prevented.

He started to lower the gun. "I'm sorry. For your pup." He damn well meant it too.

Gold mixed with the silver in Ralph's eyes. "Not nearly as sorry as you're gonna be. You really should've shot me." With a growl, he Changed into a large wolf the color of smoke.

Nik barely had time to toss the gun and Shift before the other wolf was upon him. In a tangle of fur and claws, they rolled, knocking holes into the walls and sending picture frames crashing to the floor. The two tore at each other, biting and ripping flesh until blood soaked their paws.

Ralph was tough, but he was no Alpha.

And Nik had both seen and been in plenty of dogfights.

Ralph was slow, just as his punches had been. What he had in brute force, Nik had in speed. As Ralph growled and reared back to slam his weight on top of Nik, with the intention of crushing his throat, Nik rushed forward. One rip was all it took.

Ralph's throat now gone, the other wolf sputtered and rolled on the floor until at last he lay still. As he lay dying, Ralph Shifted back into a human, no longer able to hold onto his wolf form. A smile crossed his lips. "Release," he sputtered before his chest went still.

Nik swiftly Shifted once he felt Ralph's presence leave his mind. Attacking your Alpha was an offense worthy of death.

And as Nik mulled over Ralph's last word, he suspected the other wolf had baited him so he would give him that death.

So he wouldn't have to live with the agony of knowing he'd caused the death of his only child.

Nik's fists shook on his lap.

Preventable. That was what he thought as he stared at this dead wolf, whose loss felt like a blade to his gut. Preventable and sad.

With a cry of rage, he punched a hole through the wall, not feeling the sting of splintering wood against his knuckles.

His whole body shook.

"Dammit!" he roared.

Footsteps approached, and red dots lined up on his chest.

He looked up to see Penelope and about ten armed guards from both the pack and the DPI standing nearby.

Penelope silently regarded him with those spooky silver eyes. She nodded, and the guards stepped forward.

When Nik growled, snarling and snapping at them, they paused.

"Don't make this any harder than it has to be, Nikolas," Penelope said.

"Depends on your definition of hard. And you should know better than to corner a savage beast. A wolf in bloodlust is one of the most dangerous creatures in the Underworld."

"No matter." Penelope snapped her fingers.

It felt as though someone had hit Nik upside the head with a baseball bat. Stunned as he was sent flying into the wall, he tried regaining his senses and found he couldn't move. Something burned at his wrists and ankles—silver cuffs.

They'd bound him in fucking silver.

Hissing as they hauled him to his feet, he glared at Penelope as they walked him past. "I know this isn't you, Pen, but you're a real bitch sometimes."

She smiled. "Only when I have to be. And don't worry, love." She tapped a nail under his chin. "This will all be over soon."

Then she vanished in a puff of smoke.

CHAPTER TWENTY

"TIME TO WAKE UP," A VOICE WHISPERED SOFTLY.

Alara's eyes opened. She had slept perfectly, not stirring once and rousing in the same position she'd fallen asleep in. On her back, hands clasped over her stomach, legs out straight.

The grogginess of sleep wore off quickly, giving way to sharp thinking. The room was dark; night had fallen. She must have slept for a few hours.

Her head pounded suddenly, and Alara squeezed her eyes shut and gritted her teeth.

Get. Up, Secret insisted with a growl. *Time is wasting. The ceremony has a short window of time to be performed.*

Alara tried resisting, but her soul was still too weak from the surge of magic she'd exuded earlier. *Why dusk?*

Certain times of day enhance certain types of spells. Dusk is an intersection, a crossroads from day to night. The end of one thing and the beginning of another. Perfect for a severing spell. Now move.

Getting up, Alara began getting dressed in a simple black dress and black boots. *Where are we going?* she asked as Secret directed her body to the bathroom. Her eyes were flecked with silver, and she felt like punching the mirror. How had she gotten this weak? The doppelgänger had warned her about her willpower draining away. She hadn't believed it, had thought she was strong enough.

What if she wasn't?

Secret pulled her hair up into a ponytail and attached the dagger at her hip. She didn't brush on any makeup before she turned the light off and left the suite. The guards fell in step behind her as she made her way down the stairs toward the ballroom.

Secret was silent the entire time. It made Alara antsy. *I asked you a question earlier. Where are we going?*

The ballroom.

Obviously. What for?

I told you. A spell—a sacrifice—that will save us all.

Two more guards were posted outside the doors to the rarely used ballroom. Alara had meant to reopen it, to use it for throwing grand galas as a means of reconnecting with their neighboring packs and hopefully forging stronger alliances. Only once things settled down, of course, but she had a feeling that wasn't going to be anytime soon.

The guards opened the doors for her, bowing as she floated past.

The room was lit with hundreds of candles. Everyone was there—the wolves in her pack, the DPI, even Penelope. All staring blankly at her with silver eyes, their faces void of any expression.

Like living statues.

Alara shivered, creeped out.

A circle of white and red candles had been arranged in a star in the middle of the room. And at the center of the star stood an altar, its glossy golden surface reflecting the twinkling flames.

Secret stopped behind the altar, facing the door. "Bring the sacrifice."

Alara's eyes lifted as the door opened.

And then her heart stopped.

Nik had raised hell the entire time they'd dragged his ass to the dungeon. Only they weren't going to the dungeon, he realized as a hundred glittering candles hit his line of vision and an altar came into view.

Son of a bitch. He was going to be sacrificed. Which meant the doppelgänger intended to use Blood Magic, one of the most dangerous houses of the Craft.

His eyes froze on the altar before rising to meet his mate's unwavering gaze.

"Alara," he breathed.

She clutched a dagger in her hands, her face as smooth as glass.

Struggling against his bonds, the silver burning his skin as it chafed, he growled and snapped as he was prodded forward like cattle. Penelope raised a hand, and he was lifted into the air and deposited onto the altar. Ropes appeared from nowhere, strapping him down tight. The cool metal pressed against his bare backside as he struggled but found he couldn't move. The bitch of a witch hadn't been messing around.

He glared at the doppelgänger. "What is this, some Blood Magic shit?"

It nodded, holding up the dagger. "Every sacrifice this blade has made has been out of hatred. That's how the spell cast upon it works. The hatred allows the dagger to carry the souls of whomever it's killed to Mistress Black, restoring her power. A sacrifice made out of love, however, along with a counterspell, should be enough to break Mistress Black's spell."

"How do you know that will work? Sounds like a bunch of bullshit to me."

"I've done it once before, in another witch's body. That's how I learned the spell. People have been using it to undo spells from afar for centuries, in some incarnation of magic or another."

Alara jerked her head from side to side. "No," came her quavering voice. "No, I can't do this."

Gritting its teeth, the doppelgänger seized control. "It's the only way, you fool. Don't you want to stop Mistress Black?" Closing its eyes, the doppelgänger raised its voice and spoke a few words in what sounded like Latin. The rest of the room repeated the words, bouncing back and forth from the doppelgänger to the crowd. The doppelgänger raised the dagger high, aiming the point at Nik's heart. It started to bring the dagger down, but its arm stopped.

"No!" Alara cried. "I won't let you!"

Her arm shook—she was fighting the doppelgänger.

"How… are… you still so… strong?" the doppelgänger asked. "Your will should be… weakened… by now!"

"I love him," Alara growled, her eyes briefly flashing gold through the silver. "And I won't let you take him away from me, you bitch!"

"This will stop Mistress Black! She won't be able to hurt the people you care about ever again." Its eyes found Nik's. "Don't you want to save Alara? Your pack? Your brothers?"

"No, Nik!" Alara gritted out. "Don't…listen… to it!"

The dagger inched down toward his chest, the fist gripping it turning white at the knuckles and shaking.

Nik turned the doppelgänger's words over in his head. Wasn't this what he'd been trying to accomplish all along? Save everyone he loved?

"You're bullshitting me," he said.

"I am Fey. I cannot lie."

His chest rose and fell with quicker speed as he searched his mate's beautiful face, trying to memorize it. "If I sacrifice myself, will you let Alara go?"

"Yes," it said instantly. "You have my word."

"And my pack? These people, every person under your hold?"

"They will all be released and free to live in a world safe from Mistress Black's evil whims."

He turned his head, glancing at the people surrounding him—his friends, his family, his pack.

All his life he'd worried about not being "good enough"—a good-enough leader, mate, brother, son.

Wasn't that what being a good leader was? Being

243

willing to sacrifice yourself to save your loved ones? He couldn't save Ralph; the wolf had chosen his fate. Probably because he knew in killing him, it would hurt Nik the most, being the Alpha.

If he felt Ralph's loss so deeply, then losing Alara would destroy him.

Never again. Never again will I lose another pack member.

And he had a promise to keep, the sacred oath he'd silently taken the moment he'd Marked Alara.

To protect her at any cost.

He looked into her eyes one last time.

"I love you, Alara."

Shock flitted through her face. The doppelgänger, sensing her distraction, pounced on the opportunity.

Closing his eyes, he let the dagger plunge straight into his heart.

CHAPTER TWENTY-ONE

IT FELT LIKE A BOMB HAD GONE OFF. A BLAST OF POWER swept through the air, shattering the windows, mirrors, anything else made of glass, and leveling everyone in the room.

Alara's ears rang. It was hard to focus, as though the blast of magic had scrambled her thoughts. As she sat up and waited for the room to stop spinning, she gritted her teeth against the throbbing headache pounding at her temples.

Something stirred inside of her, the doppelgänger wrought with confusion. *I don't understand,* Secret said. *It was supposed to work.*

Work. The sacrifice.

Nik.

"Oh God," Alara breathed, climbing to her feet. She nearly went down again as she stumbled her way to the lifeless body lying atop the altar. "Nik!" she screamed, cradling his head. Staring at the dagger, she almost reached for it to pull it out, but she stopped herself. There was already so much blood pouring out of the entry wound. Pulling the blade out would only make it bleed more. Trembling, she uttered her mate's name again, searching for any signs of life.

His chest barely moved, the pulse in his neck throbbing erratically.

"Nik?" she whispered.

His eyes slowly opened. Pain. There was so much pain there.

Alara felt as if she were going to break. The gravity of what she'd done threatened to crush her.

Nik started to reach for her face, his hand shaking. "I… love…" He coughed, blood spurting onto his lip as he gurgled the last word.

"I love you too." She took his hand, squeezed and kissed it. Tears poured down her face. "God, Nik, I love you so much. I'm so sorry. I'm so, so sorry."

He made a swatting motion at her cheek, wiping away her tears.

A broken smile turned the corners of his mouth up, and then he stilled.

Alara felt it, the moment his heart stopped beating.

Secret kept despairing in the back of her mind. *I don't understand. Why didn't this work? It was supposed to work! The spell… I should have felt the spell break… which means it didn't… what did I do wrong?*

Alara shook her head, staring at her mate. His skin was chilled. He was never cold, not once. Not a king of wolves.

"No," she muttered. "No, no, no, no." Her voice broke as sobs took over. "*Nik!*" she screamed, so loudly she felt her vocal cords might shatter. "*Nik!* Come back! Come back!"

The mate-bond went taut and snapped. Alara gasped at the sharp pain. It was as if her soul was being torn to pieces. The loss cut her to her core, and she wailed in agony.

It hurt. It hurt so much.

"Nik," she uttered on a broken whisper, sinking against the altar. The air was unbreathable. It stank too much of Nik's blood.

Footsteps rushed toward the room. Alara glanced backward, barely able to see through her tears. A tall man she didn't recognize but who looked oddly famil-iar stood in the doorway in nothing but jeans, sneakers, and a hoodie. A woman with long red hair stood beside him, both of them taking in the scene in horror. When her bright-green eyes found the altar, her face went pale. "Nik," she said.

Alara blinked. Did she know him?

The man's eyes followed the woman's, and sorrow flickered over his handsome features.

The people around Alara groaned as they got up, their eyes glazed over with silver.

Secret hissed. *Black Witch! Mistress Black must have caught wind of where I was and sent two of her cronies to dispose of me!*

"What?" Alara said, standing. Her eyes snapped to the

redhead, and her blood froze over. Her signature... it was similar to Secret's.

"Kill them!" Secret screeched, seizing control of Alara's vocal cords while she was distracted.

Alara fought for control over her body as the DPI and werewolves ran toward the newcomers.

The man in the doorway snarled, eyes turning gold as he lunged forward.

Alara lingered by the altar, watching as the man fought his way past one person after another. His fighting style was vicious and dirty, much like Nik's. It was impressive how lethal he was. Ducking, punching, and pummeling his way through the legion of guards, the lone werewolf held his own while the witch strolled toward Alara.

Secret hissed. "Stay back," it growled.

The woman's lovely face scrunched up in confusion. "There's something wrong with you," she mumbled, more to herself than to Alara. "What is it... Silver eyes..." Her face lit up. "Doppelgänger."

Secret roared, its fear of the witch running rampant in Alara's body. Like a cornered animal, it lashed out, throwing a blast of dark power at the witch.

The woman flung up a shield of Black Magic, seemingly on a whim. It absorbed Secret's attack and then evaporated. Those green eyes stared at her as Secret gripped the altar, stumbling alongside it, trying to find the end so it could run.

Alara seized her opportunity. "Help me!" she shouted, pleading with the witch in front of her.

Stay quiet! Secret backhanded her soul, flinging her

backward and knocking her into the wall of her consciousness. Alara struggled to get up. She was so tired. The magic had wreaked havoc on her body, like a computer whose circuits had been fried during a power surge.

The woman's green eyes lit up, glowing neon. "Get out of my sister's body," she hissed.

Alara's soul sat up. Sister?

Throwing out a hand, the woman unleashed a torrent of dark magic. The spell was unlike anything Alara had ever felt before, powerful beyond measure. The dark, shimmering vortex struck up a gale in the room, flinging furniture around and yet somehow never once disturbing Nik's corpse, which was protected by a sparkling black aura.

The magic swirled around Alara's body, caging her.

Suddenly, the witch was inside Alara's mind. The astral projection floated in the air, her bright hair hovering around her as if she were under water. Alara had never seen anything more terrifying.

Until she saw the doppelgänger.

All this time it had been nothing more than a voice, an incorporeal presence. But now her nightmares had been given form.

It was seven feet tall, at least, with limbs much too long for its body and needle-like fingers tipped in claws. Gray, shrunken skin clung to the long, thin bones of its body, which was oddly human in structure. It had no hair, just a gleaming bald scalp, like a bleached skull. Its many teeth were long and sharp and crammed together in an oval-shaped mouth that permanently gaped as a result.

Red, many-faceted eyes without lids stared at the witch in loathing.

Alara wanted to throw up. This was the thing that had been inside her?

Secret hissed at the witch. *You cannot have her! This body is mine!*

It's not her I want, the witch said, her voice booming with power. Throwing her head back and raising her arms parallel to the ground, palms up, she summoned two orbs of dark magic in either hand.

Secret shrieked, scrambling away and toward Alara.

Alara cried out, stumbling to her feet and running. A boom echoed through her mind. There was a whoosh, a scream.

With a jerk, she was flung back into her own body. Her heart hammered, and she felt cold all over, inside and out. Her pale skin was drenched in sweat, and she collapsed onto the floor.

The magical vortex around her dissipated, revealing the witch standing right in front of her, arms still held high.

The witch smiled. "There are your eyes."

Alara turned and looked at her reflection in a shard of broken glass on the floor. Her eyes were normal. The silver was at last gone. As was the malevolent presence inside her head.

With a shuddering release of breath, the witch fell to her knees, breathing heavily as she clutched at her head.

Alara started to go to her but stopped. The witch had saved her life, had destroyed the doppelgänger, but she was still a Black Witch. And with the kind of power she'd demonstrated…

Alara swallowed hard. "Thank you," she said, keeping a wary distance.

The woman smiled weakly. "Don't mention it."

All around them, bodies littered the floor, and blood saturated the air. But Nik's was the only blood she smelled.

The lone wolf hadn't killed anyone that she could see, merely knocked them out.

The fighting had stopped the moment the Black Witch destroyed the doppelgänger. Those who remained standing now shook their heads, their eyes clearing of the silvery influence of hypnosis. They looked around in confusion and panic.

Alara immediately took charge. "It's all right," she said, raising her voice, which was scratchy from screaming. She searched for her Beta, praying he was alive. Sending up silent thanks when she spotted him, she said through their pack-bond, *Keep them calm. Initiate Emergency Plan A.*

His tone was groggy, but he swiftly responded. *Yes, ma'am.*

As she watched her second-in-command take control of the situation, wrangling up the distressed wolves and DPI agents, Alara turned to find the lone wolf kneeling beside the witch. He murmured to her, stroking her face with a fierce look of love in his eyes.

She saw the tattoos Marking both of them—they were mated.

The man was shaking his head as they quietly argued, their words so soft Alara couldn't hear. At last the woman said, "I have to do this now, while the DPI is still distracted and disoriented from the spell, before they realize who we are."

"But they've already seen us."

"They've seen an illusion, an unremarkable brunette and your average Joe. I cast a disguising glamour the second we walked through the door. Don't worry." She smiled. "I got this."

The woman shrugged her mate off, stood, and walked over to the altar. Pain flickered over her face as she gazed at Nik. Placing her hands on his chest, she closed her eyes and began muttering an incantation.

Power hummed in the air, making the small hairs all over Alara's body stand up. The woman's hair lifted, her body crackling with black and purple lightning.

Alara started forward, but the man grabbed her wrist. "What is she doing?" Alara asked, glancing back at her mate with worry.

Those dark eyes regarded her solemnly, glimmering with hope. "She's trying to resurrect him."

Mistress Black felt the soul of the werewolf drawing closer. One wouldn't think of werewolves possessing much innate magical ability, but they were created from magic. The curse itself stemmed from Green Magic, and every ounce helped. She was so close to getting her old body back, could feel it in the untapped well of power flowing through her borrowed body's veins.

For the past few weeks, she'd been camped out in her

scrying room, trying to locate the Black Witch whose power had called to her own. It was the only time she'd used her magic at all, not wanting to tax herself too much when she was so close to performing the ritual that would at last restore her soul to its original body.

Thanks to the remnants of the cloaking spell her mother and mentor had placed on her, the witch had evaded her—until now.

The room was small and circular, made out of black marble. Black crystals to amplify her power sat about the scrying well in the middle of the room, an elevated pool of swirling crystalline water cupped by a bowl of silver.

Gas lamps hung from the walls. She had always preferred fire to electric bulbs. She found power and reassurance in the elements, something electricity couldn't provide.

She prepared herself to absorb the soul, waited for the breathtaking agony as the soul's life force and magic fused with her own, but it never came.

Someone had stopped the soul from coming to her.

Frowning, she reached out with her own magic, taking it easy, probing the pathway between the enchanted knife and her. The soul was stuck, as if caught in limbo. Someone was pulling it back.

"Resurrection," she breathed. Focusing on her scrying pool, she spoke an incantation that would reveal the source of the trouble. A woman with curly red hair flashed in the pool, looking so much like her dearly departed daughter, Idrina, that it hurt. And to attempt resurrection, after only coming into her powers... the girl had to be more powerful than Mistress Black had at first thought.

Gripping the edge of the pool, Mistress Black leaned over it. "Show me where she is," she commanded.

The soul slipped further away, closer to being reunited with its body. And taking any chance of finding her descendant along with it.

Tugging it back, she commanded again, "Show me where she is."

Idrina—no, Verika—yanked back, her incantation growing stronger. She was persistent. *Good.*

Mistress Black smiled, pulling harder to buy herself some more time. If she lost a soul in exchange for finding her descendant, a powerful ally, then so be it. This was so much more important than just bringing herself back right now.

Images flashed on the surface of the pool, a slideshow of clues. A forest, a Welcome to Moonstruck, Arkansas, sign along a highway, and a manor with a bronze sign out front that read, Crescent Manor, circa 1875.

Mistress Black released the soul, not wanting Verika to tax herself too much. As she'd learned at a young age, too much playing around with the power of death could bring a witch dangerously close to it herself.

No matter about the soul. She'd have another soon enough. Her subordinates had been working around the clock to bring her what she needed, and she had no doubt they would succeed very soon.

And now, at last, she'd be able to find Verika and bring her home, where she belonged.

Pleased, she started to stand, but a soul as dark as

midnight slammed into her, knocking her to her knees. This one was powerful, ancient, and wise.

A Death Fey... a doppelgänger.

Mistress Black laughed as the fire of absorbing the doppelgänger's vast magic burned through her body.

Like calls to like. One of the cardinal rules of magic.

Verika's Black Magic had recognized her own and had sent the soul of the doppelgänger to her as a gift. Oh, she probably didn't realize what she'd done, as she had only come into her power recently, but that was just fine. Mistress Black could teach her so much about her gifts.

And Verika's were many indeed. There was even a chance she was more powerful than her.

Her dark heir. With two Black Witches leading the Purging, their power would be unstoppable.

Why?

Mistress Black paused. The voice had come from inside her head, a dying plea from the doppelgänger.

Why what? she answered back.

Why... didn't it... work? So weak—it was almost gone.

Mistress Black smiled. *Oh, I knew about your little coup the moment you escaped me. Like calls to like, and you're a Death fairy. I scanned the brains of the witches you'd possessed to find out what you were after. Your little counterspell didn't work because while Alara loved Nik, your hatred for me was greater. You were the one to deliver the killing blow, not Alara.*

But it was her body!

Her body—your doing. The magic knows the difference. Thus, your hatred kept the spell intact.

An anguished wail was the doppelgänger's last sound as its power was fully absorbed.

Mistress Black sat there a minute, letting her breathing return to normal before attempting to stand. Her body vibrated with power. The doppelgänger had provided her with what she needed to finally perform the ritual.

At last—she was going to break the debilitating curse placed on her all those years ago.

And when she rose again, her first order would be to find Verika and bring her there.

CHAPTER TWENTY-TWO

"**N**ɪᴋ…"

Someone was calling his name, sounding an ocean away. The voice echoed all around him, disembodied and creepy as fuck.

"Nik!"

Louder this time. And a hell of a lot more distinct.

His heart tripped over a beat. "Alara?" He clung to the echo of that sweet voice, the hope it brought to his chest nearly making him dizzy. "Alara!" he called out.

Nothing. Fucking nothing.

Shit.

Damn.

Ba dum, ba dum, ba dum.

Where the hell was he? He looked around, not recognizing anything. Mostly because there was nothing there to recognize. It was just black. Empty.

Fuck. Was this hell? He vaguely remembered

something about a knife.

"Go."

He turned around. A blond girl stood there, her blue eyes strangely familiar.

His breath caught. "Izzy?"

"It's okay." She smiled, her delicate, pale hands clasped demurely in front of her. She wore an ice-blue dress that set off her pale skin nicely and contrasted with her fair hair. "It's not your time yet. Go to her."

They stared at one another a moment longer, and then he nodded.

"Oh, and Nik," Izzy said, stopping him. "Please tell Alara we're fine. We're all going to be just fine."

"I will." With a gruff nod, because he didn't know what the hell else to say to his mate's late sister, he took off at a dead sprint down the lone road running through the darkness.

Come on, baby, he thought. *Talk to me. Guide me.*

"Nik!" came her voice a second later.

He smiled. "Alara!"

She screamed for him again, the agony in her voice damn near unbearable.

I'm coming, baby. Wait for me. I'm coming—

He came to with a violent gasp, as if all the oxygen in the room was trying to force itself into his lungs. His chest hurt, his lungs burned. With a shaking hand, he reached up and felt the jagged scar over his heart.

Fuck. So he'd really died.

Before he could ponder the severity of that, plus the fact that he was still somehow breathing, two arms wrapped themselves around his neck in a crushing hug.

"Ow, ow, ow, ow!" he sputtered, the pain in his chest lighting up his whole torso with needle pricks.

"Sorry!" Alara said sheepishly, loosening her grip but not letting go. She might have been afraid to. Those gray eyes he adored so much stared at him openly in disbelief.

He touched the skin beside her eyes softly. "You're you. What happened to the doppelgänger?"

"It's gone. It's been destroyed." She gently caressed his face. "You're here."

"I'm here." He grasped her hand and held it. "And I'm back to stay."

Some things words just couldn't do shit for. Pulling his mate to him, he kissed her deeply, pouring all the love and tenderness he felt for her into his lips. She closed her eyes and embraced him back, the two of them locked in their own little world until someone cleared their throat behind them.

Fuck 'em. They could wait. Coming up for air, he immediately went in to kiss her again, but he noticed her cheeks were shiny. "Aw, baby," he said, wiping at the hot tears. "Why are you crying?"

"Because... I... killed you," she sobbed. "I don't know how you can stand to look at me."

"Sssh. It wasn't your fault. Nothing that's happened has been your fault." He cupped her face, stared into her eyes. "I told you I would die for you when you made me the happiest wolf alive by becoming my mate. And I'd gladly do it again, over and over."

"Oh, Nik." She kissed him. "I love you."

"I love you too, baby. More than you'll ever know."

He held her, stroked her silky hair, took in her scent.

His Alara. He finally had her back.

An immense sense of relief went through him, making him feel a hundred pounds lighter.

"Oh, before I forget," he said. "Your sister wanted me to tell you something. She said to tell you, 'We're fine. We're all going to be just fine.'"

Alara stilled. A smile, small but hopeful, broke through her tears.

"Ahem."

"What?" Nik growled, finally looking up to see who the hell was annoying him. He blinked, and the glamour masking the strangers' faces fell away for a few seconds.

Nik didn't recognize the bastard at first. Tall, built, same cocky-ass grin he wore half the time. Eyes like their mother's, blue as the sky. Hair blacker than midnight.

E-Elijah?

Behind him stood a woman that knocked the breath out of Nik, her fiery hair glowing in the light of the fireplace behind her. She met his eyes, blushed, and looked away. "Nice to see you again, Nik," she said quietly.

"Verika," he breathed.

Alara's eyes widened as they flashed to the witch. A low growl sounded in her throat, and Nik pulled her closer, soothing her. Astounded as he was at seeing his ex, that was all it was—surprise. No regret they weren't together, no spark of affection for his lost love.

No, the love for his mate had overshadowed his puppy love for Verika long ago.

He looked at Verika's hands, which she jerked behind her. He caught a flash of blue ink, shimmering in the firelight.

Eyes narrowing, he swiftly looked at Elijah's neck. The tips of a swirling tattoo peeked above the collar of his shirt.

Nik's eyes widened. "No. Fucking. Way." He rose to his feet. "Be right back, baby," he said, kissing Alara's hand. "There's something I've gotta do."

His eyes flashed gold as he rounded on Elijah, who flashed him a guilty smile.

"Hello, brother," Elijah said, lifting a hand to wave.

It never made it.

BAM!

Elijah's head jerked back as Nik's fist introduced itself to his jaw. *Motherfucker.* Showing his face in his house, mating to his ex, of all people.

Verika gawked at him as she went to her mate. The asshat had stumbled but not fallen.

Tch. Not surprising. If Nik remembered correctly, the jerk had a rough reputation. Liked to fight almost as much as Nik did.

Then he probably wouldn't mind a few more hits.

Nik cracked his knuckles, closing in, but Verika swiftly stepped in his way.

"Move," he growled.

"No." Verika glared at him. "He helped save your life. You should be hugging him, not punching him."

"It's the universal greeting for assholes."

"Really, Nik?" Verika put her hands on her hips. "You're acting like a child now? With everything that's at stake?"

"Don't start with me," Nik said, though he took a step back. Otherwise, he wouldn't be held responsible if his fist happened to fly out and clock Elijah in the jaw again.

His brother stood behind his mate, staring at the floor, a hard expression on his face. He rubbed his jaw where Nik had hit him.

Nik looked away, unable to stand the sight of him. A tidal wave of hurt slammed into him.

Why hadn't he called?

Why hadn't he visited?

Why hadn't he cared?

Elijah had a lot to answer for, but first, Verika was right. They had bigger problems.

Nik stalked around, restless, surveying the damage in the room. No dead people, he noted with relief. From out in the hallway, he could hear his Beta directing their pack-mates and Agent Asshat demanding answers and threatening to lock them all up for treason.

Ah, the life of an Alpha. Duty never ended.

"I'll deal with you later," Nik said, flinging a glare at Elijah, who glared right back.

With a growl of annoyance, Nik flipped his Alpha switch and stalked toward the hallway.

Being brought back from the dead gave you a fresh perspective on life. Like how much it meant to you, for starters.

In the predawn hours, Nik had gotten up from bed,

careful not to disturb his sleeping mate, and gone to the balcony for some fresh air.

Sorting out the mess with the hypnotized DPI and his bewildered pack had taken hours. Luckily, one of the DPI agents was magic savvy enough to get the reenactment spell to work—all except the resurrection part. Nik suspected Verika was to thank for the spell suddenly going hazy and cutting out, but he couldn't blame her. She had to cover up any evidence of her being there, considering both she and Elijah were wanted by the DPI.

The rest of the spell went off without a hitch and would have been cool if it weren't so damn weird. Ghostly figures of the agents and his pack had reenacted the events in the ballroom. Watching his mate stab him in the heart was creepy, but Nik was a big wolf. Agent Chang looked as if he'd swallowed a turd as he watched himself, complete with freaky silver eyes, participate in the ritual. He didn't seem as eager to beat around the bush this time as he interrogated everyone present—all except Verika and Elijah. As soon as the bewitched agents snapped out of the doppelganger's spell, Verika had whipped up an invisibility shield and gotten her and her mate out of there, pronto. Nik, using the telepathic blood-bond with his brother, had discreetly directed them to a hiding spot until the DPI had left.

The paramedics were horrified to find out they'd killed their partner. As they took care of Amber's body, Nik felt a stab of guilt.

Was there something more he could have done?

Nah. He knew there wasn't, that it was survivor's

remorse. He felt bad as hell for that paramedic who'd delivered the killing blow. He could tell the guy was eaten up with guilt.

Sometime late into the night, Chang had released them and said he'd find Nik if he had more questions. Fine by him. Nik took the opportunity to bounce. After the DPI had completely vacated the premises, he'd grabbed Elijah, Verika, and Alara and headed into his office for a chat. And by chat, he meant demanding answers, starting with what the hell had happened while he was dead. He couldn't overhear Alara talking to the police over all the noise in the room, but he knew she'd lied to cover up the fact that Elijah and Verika had been there at all. She'd said something about still being under the doppelganger's control and not remembering anything at that point.

After Verika had explained to Nik what had gone down and how she'd brought him back, he'd been speechless.

For starters, Verika—sweet, bookish, unassuming little Verika—was a Black Witch.

Secondly, he'd fucking died. He knew he had, but it just hadn't sunk in until now. As if he was in shock and the denial had just worn off. And once it did, shit got real, fast.

And thirdly, his brother was back, dragging along Nik's old flame as his mate. His mind was still trying to process that one.

Fate sure had an odd sense of humor.

Verika had quickly explained her and Elijah's backstory, including how they'd met, how she'd found out she had Black Magic, and why they were there. Elijah had kept silent the whole time, stealing glances at Nik and quickly looking away when Nik caught him.

He still didn't know what to make of his older brother's return. While he wanted to feel overwhelmed with joy, there was a larger part of him that was pissed as hell.

Where the hell have you been, Elijah? Why now?

He was so not looking forward to that chat, which would inevitably turn into a brawl. They'd be lucky if one of them didn't end up killing the other.

"Fuck," he breathed, running his hands through his hair.

"We could do that, if it would help relieve the stress," came a suggestive voice from the door.

Nik smiled.

There stood his mate, clad in only a bedsheet.

He let his eyes sweep her down and up as she joined him. "It appears we've already done that, but I'm certainly open to doing it again."

She smiled and kissed his shoulder.

He pulled her to him, wrapping his arm around her and holding her close. "Feeling better?"

"A little. It will take a long time to get over what I've done, to forgive myself."

He nodded. "I'll be here."

She hugged him, resting her head on his shoulder. "What are you going to do about Elijah? And Verika?"

Her voice tripped over the woman's name. "You have nothing to fear from her being here," he said, kissing her hair. "I'm totally over her."

"I trust you," she said, inhaling deeply and sighing it out. "But a girl can't help but wonder. The 'great, lost love' and all."

"You're my great love."

"As you are mine."

He growled in approval, smiling as he rested his cheek against her satiny hair. "To answer your question about Eli, I don't know. A lot of time has passed. I don't know if I can forgive him—or trust him."

"But you hope to."

He looked down. "Did that doppelgänger make you telepathic?"

"Nope. I'm just taking advantage of that mate-bond I've missed so much." She shivered. "I do owe Verika a thank you for ridding me of that thing."

That made two of them. Nik would forever be indebted to that witch for saving his mate, and his own life.

The favors and IOUs were just stacking up, weren't they?

"Do you really think Elijah knows how to find Mistress Black?" Alara asked. She'd been present earlier when Nik had grilled Verika over how they had come to be at the manor. He could tell she'd minced Eli's backstory, but that was fine. It was his to tell, and someday Nik would hear it.

"If he's spent time with her, it's definitely a possibility."

"We can't fight her alone."

"No. We'll need help. We should reunite the packs, call in any favors owed from other races. War is coming." He frowned, throwing a challenging glare at the lightening horizon. "And it's damn well time we finished this."

END OF BOOK FIVE

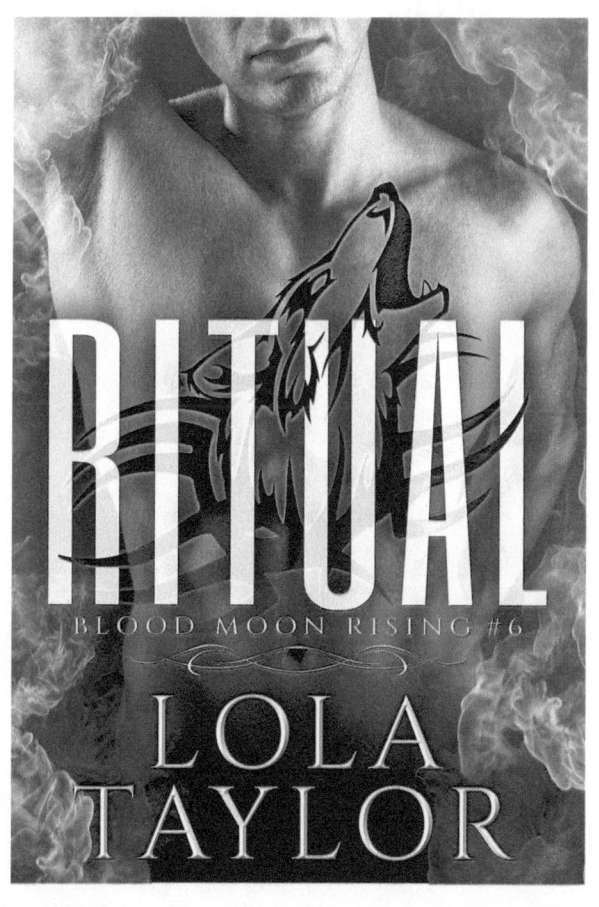

The final battle is here! Look out for *Ritual*,
the explosive conclusion to the Blood Moon
Rising series.
Now available!

OTHER BOOKS BY
LOLA TAYLOR

The Her Dark Desires Trilogy
Carnal (free for a limited time!)
Sinful
Soulful (coming soon!)

Blood Moon Rising
Fever (free for a limited time!)
Protector
Betrayal
Captured
Sacrifice
Ritual

Blood Moon Rising companion novels
Lust
Forever (coming soon!)

Standalone novels
Shatter

For a full list of titles, please visit
www.lolataylorbooks.com.

For more information, please visit
www.lolataylorbooks.com

Your opinion matters—please leave a review!

Thank you for reading my book! If you have a moment, I'd really appreciate an honest rating and review. They help authors stand out in a busy marketplace, plus they give browsing readers the nitty-gritty on books they're shopping. Everyone wins when you rate and review, so please do! Your opinion counts!

"Lola Taylor" is a pen name created for the romances I can't show my grandma without blushing. My favorite genre to write is romantic suspense, usually involving hot werewolves, warlocks, or any other type of paranormal creature. Keep the action hot and the romance hotter—that's my motto! I'm a horror film junkie, I still love Halloween as an adult (seriously, I think I get more excited for it than some kids do), and what precious spare time I have is spent with my family, reading (everything from sci fi to middle grade), playing the flute, painting pretty pictures, or screwing around on Pinterest or Etsy. Hailing from the South, I currently live in the Midwest with five fur babies and my hubby.

You can connect with me on Facebook (www.facebook.com/lolataylorbooks) or my email (lolawritespnr@gmail.com). Learn more about me and my books at www.lolataylorbooks.com.